Anonymous

Hugh Russell at Harrow

A Sketch of School Life

Anonymous

Hugh Russell at Harrow
A Sketch of School Life

ISBN/EAN: 9783337013509

Printed in Europe, USA, Canada, Australia, Japan

Cover: Foto ©Raphael Reischuk / pixelio.de

More available books at **www.hansebooks.com**

HUGH RUSSELL AT HARROW.

A SKETCH OF SCHOOL LIFE.

BY

AN OLD HARROVIAN.

"Forty years on, when afar and asunder,
   Parted are those who are singing to-day,
 When you look back, and forgetfully wonder
 What you were like in your work and your play,
 Then, it may be, there will often come o'er you,
 Glimpses of notes like the catch of a song,
 Visions of boyhood shall float them before you,
 Echoes of dreamland shall bear them along."

SCHOOL SONG.

London:

PROVOST AND CO.,

40, TAVISTOCK STREET, COVENT GARDEN.

——

1880.

PREFACE.

HE writing of this little book has been the occupation of a period of enforced confinement to the house, and has re-called to the Author many a pleasant memory.

Those who take up this book, expecting to find it an exciting narrative, or a highly finished picture of school life, with delicately drawn characters, will, it is feared, be very greatly disappointed. It pre-tends to be nothing more than a *rough* sketch of life at Harrow, while the characters are at best but mere shadowy *outlines*.

It should once for all be stated that it has been the Author's aim to avoid taking, so to speak, the portrait of any Harrovian, past or present, in the pages of this book, and his readers are assured that by "Mr. Kingsford's," no house in particular is meant.

The glossary (for the use of any non-Harrovian readers who may look at this book) cannot lay claim to be by any means a complete vocabulary of Harrow slang; still the Author ventures to hope that it will fulfil its purpose.

The Author's thanks are due to an old Harrovian for several valuable suggestions, and other aids.

CONTENTS.

CHAP.		PAGE
I.	FIRST IMPRESSIONS	9
II.	HOUSE LIFE...	16
III.	EASTER TERM	24
IV.	RUNNING EXPERIENCES...	30
V.	CONCERNING WORK	38
VI.	SUMMER TERM	43
VII.	COUSIN CHARLIE	51
VIII.	THE "EX"	61
IX.	COCK-HOUSE MATCH	68
X.	TRIALS	74

CHAP. PAGE

XI. RATS 84

XII. DECORATIONS 90

XIII. ANOTHER SUMMER TERM 96

XIV. LORDS 103

XV. RUSSELL'S "FIND" 105

XVI. A "STOPPED EX" 116

XVII. SIXTH-FORM DIGNITY 124

XVIII. CONCLUSION 131

HUGH RUSSELL AT HARROW.

CHAPTER I.

FIRST IMPRESSIONS.

"My boy, th' unwelcome hour is come,
When thou, transplanted from thy genial home,
Must find a colder soil and bleaker air,
And trust for safety to a stranger's care."

COWPER.

NE September afternoon a fly might have been seen crawling up the hill from the Harrow station. Outside was a portmanteau, a hamper, and a large wooden box; inside, a hat-box, a large bag, an umbrella, and a small boy. The fly drew up before the front door of one of the masters' houses. With some diffidence, the small boy, after extricating himself from his baggage, proffered the flyman three shillings, but was promptly informed by that worthy that six was always the fare. What was the good of arguing?

the door opened, and Mr. Kingsford, a kind-looking
elderly man, advanced and shook hands, saying, " I
remember your father well; he was in this house
many years ago, when I was one of the junior
masters, and an honour he was to it, in work and
play alike." Then after a few inquiries about his
parents, he moved towards the door, saying, " I'll
introduce you to the matron, Miss Browne, and then
you can find out your room, and so on, before the
rush of fellows comes. They don't return till the
evening generally—like to make the very most of
their holidays, you know."

In a few moments our hero was sitting in a snug
little room, discussing a cup of tea with a pleasant
old lady. He did not know it then, but Miss Browne
had quite a mania for offering tea to her guests, and
was deeply offended if they would not take any,
whether it was morning, noon, or night. " Now,
my dear boy," she began, as if she had known him
all her life, " I may as well take the opportunity to
give you a few words of advice about several things
which you will find it hard to resist in this place.
They will ask you—nay, command you—to play at
football, whether it is wet or fine, and whether you
are well or not. My dear boy, *never you play football*
except on nice fine, warm days, and always wear
your thickest coat and comforter, both in going down
and coming up. Then again, *never be led into playing*
rackets ; it is a dangerous game. Last term a boy
in this house slipped and fell; and though he did
not hurt himself outwardly, yet the shock to his
nervous system was so great that he was unable to
resume his studies for a week." Much more whole-
some warning did the good old lady administer, and

to hear her, few would have thought how keen she really was for the honour of the house, and how on the day of a "house-match" she would hurry down through the mud, and stay from beginning to end, hardly restraining herself from shouting when a base was gained.

"Your room is No. 10," she said, after her little lecture was ended; "it is a dormitory with five beds, but in a term or two you will get put into one of the regular rooms with the cupboard beds, and only one boy besides yourself, where you will be more comfortable. At present your sitting-room will be with Adams and Drake senior, in No. 7." So saying, she rang the bell, which was answered by a maid-servant who conducted Russell to No. 10, where we will leave him to unpack and secure for himself the snuggest of the five beds before any one else arrives.

Passing over the events of the following day, which for our hero were unimportant—a French examination taking place in the afternoon—let us imagine ourselves in No. 10 early the next morning. All except one, Burton by name, are new fellows, and they are all naturally, except him (for he has no chance of a remove), rather anxious to know their places in the school. Although none of the four (for number five has not turned up yet) had ever seen each other till the night before last, they seem very good friends. "Wonder when we've got to get up," said Russell, drowsily; then, raising his voice, "I say, Burton, what time did you say 'Speecher' was?" "O bother you," exclaimed that party, who was trying to doze, "can't you let a fellow take his 'froust' the very second morning? I believe it's at eight, at least it usually is." To hear him talk you

would think Burton had been three or four years at
Harrow, whereas really he was only one term old.
Suddenly a bell begins, an impatient-sounding, rest-
less bell, and at its sound Russell and the two other
new fellows, Vernon and Leigh, jump out of bed,
thinking they are late. "You'd better get up,
Burton," says one of them, "bell is going!" (this
from the depths of a basin of cold water). No answer. "I say, you fellow, you'll be late!" cries
another, as he hurries on his clothes. "No fear,"
replies the veteran, "only first bell!" It is provoking, but as they are so far dressed, it is no good
going to bed again, so after completing their toilet,
they saunter downstairs, encountering numbers of
sleepy fellows in their nightshirts rushing to the hot
water tap with jugs.

By the time the three reach the school-yard a
sprinkling of fellows is beginning to collect, while
every few minutes a master sweeps up the street in
cap and gown. In a few moments the sprinkling
becomes a crowd, and the crowd a crush, as every one
hurries up the steps into the old speech-room. Here
the new fellows crowd into the space under the
gallery, behind the masters, known as the "sheep-
pen." A great hum of voices and trampling of feet
fill the room, but as the clock strikes, a sudden
silence takes place. Then, after prayers, the head
master rises to read the new order for the term, beginning at the bottom of the school. How many
hearts are beating! Fellows try to look indifferent, but it is a time of suspense for not a few.
Russell listens, visibly anxious, as he hears the lists
of the Third and Second Fourth forms read, then the
Upper Fourth. "New boys in the Upper Fourth

form," continues the head master, "Leigh, Vernon,
—— " Ah ! there are his companions, but still not
Russell. At last it comes ; he is in the Middle Shell.
He cannot help turning to his neighbour to ask if
he too has been read out; but one of the masters
turns in his seat and frowns, so our hero is hushed
into silence.

Soon after, he finds himself following his new
master to his schoolroom, where a short time is
spent in giving out the work for the term, and preparation for eleven o'clock school, after which the
form disperses. Burton is in this form, and he at
once pounces upon Russell for a promise to do his
work with him.

After breakfast in the hall, Russell strolls up town
to post a letter, and coming back he meets several
of his old schoolfellows, who all seem to envy him
the lofty position he has taken in the school.

Nothing remarkable took place that day, but next
morning our hero met with a little adventure that is
perhaps worth recording.

Hearing that he was in Mr. ——'s " Teek Div.,"
and that the exercise was such-and-such a number
in " Colenso," he studiously worked out the sums
overnight, and next morning repaired in his in-
nocence to his form room. On entering the room,
he found his form master surrounded by a lot of big
fellows, so he beat a hasty retreat. He asked some
one who was standing outside where he ought to go
to, but this fellow happened to be a wag, so he sent
him to a room under the "Vaughan," where he
disturbed a form that was just beginning work.
Altogether it was late before, with the help of
"Noggs," he found his way into a dingy attic, at

the very top of the old schools. Everybody turned at his entrance, and the master stopped writing on the black-board to ask his name and what made him so late. " Speak to me afterwards," he said, as our hero began to stammer out an explanation. The " speaking" consisted in a " pun " of fifty lines, for absenting himself from " Fourth-form prayers," an institution the existence of which he was altogether ignorant.

However, after a few such little mistakes and troubles, Russell shook down into his new life, and before a week had passed, found himself rarely at a loss as to what he ought to do, and where he ought to go to. Altogether, as he wrote in a letter home, he liked Harrow very much, and got to know some very nice fellows, and he was sure he should be very happy.

CHAPTER II.

HOUSE LIFE.

"The Alps and the white Himalayas
Are all very pleasant to see ;
But of right little, tight little, bright little hills,
Our Harrow is highest, say we."

SCHOOL SONG.

R. KINGSFORD's house numbered about 40. The head of the house during Russell's first year was Hawkins, a monitor, and in both house elevens, being captain of the football. The cricket captain was Belfield, a fellow rather low down in the school, but very good at games, and in the school cricket eleven. He was a general favourite, having made cock-score at Lord's last summer, and thus contributing in no small degree to a glorious victory. "Jimmy" was the name he usually went by—nobody knew why, as his real name was Arthur. The two other notabilities in the house were Brydges, who was captain of the School Rifle Corps, and mad about recruiting ; and Charlton, the great "swot," not that he did "swot" so very much, but he was very clever, and very young.

He was second in the house, being in the Upper Sixth; he had won nearly all the school medals, scholarships, and prizes, and was altogether a regular prodigy, looked upon as a certain senior wrangler of the future.

Fagging was by no means as formidable as Russell had expected. He was "find-fag" to Brydges' "find," consisting of four, and as the party almost always went up town for their own hot meat, and rarely had company, he had very little to do, beyond filling the tea-pot and clearing away.

"Day-boy" was a less trivial post, especially if his day fell in the week when he was also find-fag. Lighting and attending to all the Sixth-form fires, running messages, filling seven baths after "footer," taking the balls up to be blown; all these duties were a little burdensome. The fire-lighting bothered him most: very little wood, no paper, and lots of coal-dust were his materials, and as fast as he lighted one fire, an irate Sixth-form fellow would enter to demand why *his* had been allowed to go out; then he found it was ten o'clock, "pupe-time," after which he had school till dinner-time. In those unmerciful days the day-boy was not excused footer, and he had all the Sixth-form baths to fill afterwards. Then, afternoon school—probably a row with his master, owing to his having had no time to prepare his work. Then all the evening had to be spent in endeavouring to relight the defunct fires, without wood or paper, while for his negligence in letting them go out, he was probably "put on" for an extra day or two.

He tried several dodges to lighten his work, such as "tipping" one of the servants to keep the fires going while he was "up," and laying in a large stock of patent fire-lighters from the "Harrow Stores," but both these systems proved expensive, and did not answer as well as he expected, since the menial was in the employ of others besides himself, and the fire-lighters, which he secreted under his bed, were usually bagged in his absence by unscrupulous fellows, who appreciated a good fire. Still there was not that amount of hardship and physical pain to be endured which outsiders usually associate with the mention of fagging at a public school ; and if a racket did occasionally appear on the scene, what a hero and a martyr did the negligent fag appear among his equals.

Of course, during his first term, Russell was of no great importance, except in his own little circle of acquaintance, chiefly consisting of those who had come with him into the school ; and in those good old days no new fellow ever thought of whistling about the passages, or skylarking at the house-door, or if he did, he was soon taught his position. With very few exceptions, the only big fellows he knew to speak to were Adams and Drake senior, in whose room he sat, or rather stood, for it was one of those untidy sort of rooms where a chair is never to be found, being either broken or borrowed, so that our hero did most of his work either standing, kneeling, or sitting on the edge of the coal-scuttle.

The occupants of No. 7 rejoiced in the possession of an electric machine, with which they delighted to administer shocks to the uninitiated. Of course Russell was usually the subject of their experiments, which he underwent with exemplary submission and good-nature. One night, Adams and Drake applied the machine to their door handle, in the expectation

of surprising the servant who came to see the lights
out: by and by steps were heard down the passage; the
handle was turned—a pause—a struggle—a cry as
of some one in pain. The conspirators with difficulty
restrained their laughter. The plan had succeeded
beyond expectation. In a minute or two the com-
passionate Drake said, " Come now, the poor fellow
has had enough of it ; let him go ! " So they " broke
the connection," as they called it, and awaited the
entrance of the irate servant. The door opened and
in walked— *the House-master*, not a little nettled at
the joke which had been played on him! He threat-
ened to forfeit the machine. Drake and Adams
pleaded their love of scientific research, but he didn't
seem to see it, and, repeating his threat, left the
room, after giving the science-loving pair a Georgic
apiece. The machine was eventually taken from
them, being the result of an experiment on a small
terrier belonging to the " private side."

After this misfortune the philosophers invested in
an air-pistol, with which they practised target-shoot-
ing at the door panel, to the danger of anybody
coming suddenly into the room ; but one day one of
the darts narrowly missing the eye of one of the
maids, she made a complaint, which resulted in the
abstraction of the weapon.

Adams was in the Third Fifth, and Drake in the
Upper Remove, though, by reason of his stature, he
wore " tails,"—" Charity tails," as Adams called
them ; but Drake was highly offended if he heard such
a thing said. " Can't you fellows understand," he
would say, " that ' *Charity-tails* ' are only when
fellows *below* the Removes stick on tails ; in the
Removes they are ' *Voluntary-tails*,' put on at the will

of the wearer; nobody can stop his having them."
To this doctrine Drake stuck, and never lost an
opportunity of impressing it on his friends. In
consequence of this he obtained the nickname of
" Tails," which clung to him ever after.

One Saturday evening Russell came into No. 7
with a pensive air, and stopped before his book-shelf
for about five minutes before he took down an atlas,
and, placing it on the table, drew up the coal-scuttle
and settled himself to turn over its leaves. By and
by he began rather timidly, " Oh, Adams, are you very
busy?" " No," replied Adams, who was concocting
a brew over the fire, "what is the row?" " Well,
I've got a beastly map to do, and I've never done
one before, and I don't know how to set about it."
" Oh, I'll soon show you," replied Adams, jumping
up, and upsetting the brew into the fire in his haste :
"have you got any cardboard?" " No." " Well
then, go and borrow a bit." In a few minutes
Russell returned with the required article. " Now
then," said Adams, " what map is it?" " India."
" All right, capital ; you ought to trace it by rights,
but this will do as well." So saying, he dashed off
an outline (in the shape of a V slightly rounded at
the bottom), drew a wavy line or two for the chief
rivers, and then said, " Fill my tooth-glass with
water, while I go and bag somebody's paints!" In
a few minutes he returned with a paint-box and a
brush, and proceeded to render the map gaudy, if not
artistic. " Now then, the rest you can do yourself.
Just run a pen over the rivers I have marked in
pencil, then put in half a dozen big towns from the
atlas, and fill up any blank or bare-looking places,
with small rivers, lakes, mountains, and towns."

With this parting advice, and the request to "keep
the fire going, I shan't be back till prayers," he went
off to spend the evening in a room downstairs, where
on Saturday nights the members of a "Biscuit and
Cocoa Club" were wont to congregate.

Russell went on quietly with his map. In a few
minutes Drake came in and settled himself in a
"frouster" which he had bagged from the next room.
"Map?" he asked laconically. "Yes," replied Russell. Then a silence, only interrupted by the scratching of the pen on the map, and the occasional
dropping of a coal from the fire. At last; "I say;
this part of the map looks so bare, what shall I do?"
"Oh, stick in towns!" "But there aren't any in
the atlas within miles." "Well, never mind, I'll
tell you some. India is it? Very well, fire away!
Botherabad, Humbugee, Punchistan, Walloppore,
Fiddleabad—any more?" "No, thanks, that'll do.
Now about these mountains; I don't know how to
draw them." "Oh, I'll try and help you," said
Drake, getting up and seizing the pen. "Look here,
like a caterpillar, so, you know, or else——" "Oh,
I say," interrupted the learner, "you've put a range
right across where the mouths of the Ganges come!"
"Oh, have I? what's the odds? you can cut through,
or go round the other side, or don't bother about the
Ganges at all; but, as I was saying, there's another
way—in fact, several—of doing mountains. Besides
the caterpillar-pattern there's the zigzag; just back-
wards and forwards like this" (drawing a chain of
mountains promiscously in the sea), "and then
there's the coal dodge, very effective, see; it ought
really to be done with a stump, but this does quite
as well," and so saying. he seized a bit of coal,

moistened it, and proceeded to make a grimy line
with his little finger, having first rubbed it on the
coal. Russell was much obliged, but declined to
learn any more ways of doing mountains—three separate styles on one map (including a range in the sea,
to contain which he had to draw an imaginary island)
were quite enough, so at least thought the master
to whom the production was shown up.

"House-singing" was not very delightful to Russell in these younger days, as his voice was n··t
melodious, which was a very good reason why he
should always be "put on" for a solo, which amused
others more than himself. He didn't mind it so
much when it was in the house, but when they joined
other houses down in the music-room (as they did
then every other week), the publicity became rather
trying. Besides this, he had (as a new fellow) to
attend compulsory singing on half-holiday afternoons,
so altogether for him music had but few charms.
With regard to this compulsory class-singing we may
notice a little incident not altogether pleasant.

The first whole holiday that our hero spent at
Harrow, he "cut" singing in the afternoon. Next
day his name was read out at first school to go to the
head master at nine o'clock. He couldn't imagine
why he had been "sent up," and of course everybody grinned and went through an absurd panto-
mime strongly suggestive of corporal punishment.
At nine o'clock he made his way to the head master's
room for the dreaded interview. When he was
charged with absenting himself from singing, his
indignation was very great. His line of argument
was—singing is looked on as a lesson; a holiday is
a day when no lessons are done; *therefore* there is no

singing on a whole holiday. But the head master failed to see it in the same light, and dismissed him with a hundred Greek lines.

From the very first, our hero had gone in for "footer" with a will. He refused to take advantage of the respite customary to new fellows, and every house-game saw him down. At "compul." he was very regular too, and he was a most enthusiastic spectator at house matches.

In the latter his house had been singularly fortunate, and succumbed only in "cock-house match," on which occasion Russell spent all his "allows," and the remainder of his pocket-money, on lemons, for the gallant players of his house, and was hoarse for days after from shouting.

Another pastime in which he indulged a good deal was "squash-rackets." There was a very good "squash-court" attached to the house, and whenever he could get a "place," Russell was to be seen there.

And so, it will be seen, our hero's first time was by no means unhappy, and when the Christmas holidays began, he drove down to the station with a half-feeling of reluctance to part from his friends, even for a few weeks, so pleasantly had the time passed.

CHAPTER III.

EASTER TERM.

"It was not many days beyond the Feast of Valentine,
When to be a gallant Torpid I fervently did pine."
FROM "THE HARROVIAN."

"OT your remove?" said Hawkins, the head of Russell's house, touching our hero on the shoulder. "Yes; just scraped through, only one below me." It was the second morning of the Easter term, after "Speecher," and Russell happened to be in the hot-meat room at Winkley's when Hawkins came in. It was a cold morning, and the place was crowded. "Six of sausages, without!" gently suggested the modest Fourth-form boy. "Now then, look sharp, three bob of steak and cutlets!" roared the impatient representative of a hungry "find." "I've been here this last hour!" cried some one who had just stepped in—"a bob of fish-cutlets with!" "Oh, I say, it's no good waiting, come round to the eggs-and-bacon place," said another to his companion. It seemed as if Russell would never get the meat for his "find."

At last he got it, and started off at a run along the street, As he neared the house, he heard "Bo-o-o-o-o-oy," and recognised Brydges' call. He hurried upstairs, and found the "find" in a great state of impatience. "Why was he so late? Had he been able to get salmon? Had he brought rolls?" As soon as he had answered these questions satisfactorily, and made the tea, he hurried down to hall, to partake of his own meal, but had hardly sat down before he heard another call from Brydges. What had he forgotten? he wondered. Salt? No. Mustard? No. There was nothing for it but to go; so he left his "six of sausages" untouched, and ran upstairs. "What is it?" he breathlessly inquired, putting his head in at the door. "Come in," said Brydges solemnly. (No hope of his getting down before the breakfast in the hall was cleared.) "I have put down your name," continued Brydges, "for the Rifle Corps, and I am going to tell you what you are expected to do." So saying, he proceeded to describe the various drills, practices, &c., which were necessary to be attended. This was all very well, and no doubt it was a great honour to be thus familiarly instructed by the captain of the corps; still, to be enlisted without his knowledge, was too much of a good thing. However, resistance was useless; the considerate captain had ordered the tailor to come and measure Russell and several others for their uniforms, and had had their names duly entered. So Private Russell resolved to make the best of it, and before long was very proud of his military position; and he was most industrious in persuading his friends to join the corps.

Before long " Torpids " began, and Russell played
for his house. In their first tie they were easily
successful, but in the next draw they were confronted
with a very good team, and played a game worth
recording.

Great was the excitement among the players on
the eventful day. Russell played " half-back," which
was not his usual place, a change having been
caused by one of the "torpids " having got hurt in the
last match. He was therefore, naturally, not a little
nervous. For the first quarter of an hour the ball
was kept well down by the enemy's base, but at last
Irving (the captain of the other side, and a "fez")
got hold of it, and began a smart " run-up." On
he came like the wind, keeping the ball close in front
of him, dodging first one and then another. He
was a big heavy fellow, and Russell didn't like the
looks of him. However, he saw that he must tackle
him, and accordingly prepared to charge him. Of
course it was like running against a house, but still
it checked his progress ; and before he had recovered
himself, Russell had picked himself up, and was
taking the ball down the side. Irving was soon up
with him, and " skied " him, but not before our hero
had sent the ball flying right down to the other end,
where, after a little knocking about, it soon found its
way between the poles. It was the only base gained
that day, and the victory was considered as in a great
measure due to Russell's plucky play. In the next
tie he played " forward," and had the satisfaction of
getting a base himself.

It will be remembered that he had secured his
remove, but the increase of work was not burdensome. However, somehow he was not so high in

week's order as he wished, and this term he found
his way into the realms of "extra." Not that he
became a regular denizen of the room over Old
Speecher, one of those phlegmatic mortals who
turn up there every time as regular as clock-work,
and who know exactly what master is taking
"extra," and whether it is safe to eat apples or
chocolate under his nose. Russell went to "extra,"
but only twice that term, and he failed to form the
attachment to that institution which some regular
goers profess.

Time passed quickly, and the races were soon on.
New fellows, as a rule, do not go out running much,
nor was Russell an exception. However, he started
in all the house races, getting second in the "small
hundred;" and managing to pull off the half-mile,
owing in some measure to his good handicap.

His house did not have house sports, an institution now kept up by only one or two houses; but
they had a house steeple-chase, in which everybody,
big and small, started; all, except a few of the
older fellows, going head first into the water-jump,
which the late rains had swelled. In this race our
hero had the misfortune to hurt his ankle, which
laid him up in "sicker" for a little time. However,
he didn't mind, as he saw plenty of company, and
had no work to do.

One evening, as he was lying reading a book,
during Fourth school-time, he heard somebody coming upstairs, and in a moment Burton entered the
room. "Hullo!" said Russell, "I thought you
were up in school." "So I ought to be," he replied, "but I've only just got out of 'pupe.'"
"What? why it's half an hour since Fourth school

began!" " Yes, I know, but I left my hat in
'pupe,' and ran back to fetch it, and while I was
there, the 'old man' (Mr. Kingsford) came to lock
the door, which he had forgotten to do; I sung out,
but he didn't hear, and so I've been bottled up there
ever since." "How did you get out?" "Oh,
Hopper came in to see about the fire" (Hopper was
one of the footmen), "and after being nearly frightened
out of his life on seeing me, he released me. As
it is, I've 'cut' school, so I may as well set to and
do some of my poetry for to-night. Help me, there's
a good fellow." So saying, he got out a pen, and,
after finding a piece of paper, said: "Now; English
verses on Magna Charta; come, give us an idea."
"Well," said Russell, after pondering a few minutes,
"couldn't you begin something like this :—

"O glorious Magna Charta,
    The noble and the——"

"No, that won't do; try something else, something
about King John." After some deliberation they
produced between them the following spirited lines,
with which I will conclude this chapter.

THE MAGNA CHARTA.

King John did sit upon his throne
In famous London town,
When nobles did a glorious deed
For signature bear down.
The king he sat, and held his pen,
And smiled so bland around;
And smiled again, and called for ink,
And made a pleasing sound :
A sound of laughter and of mirth,
Whereat all did applaud,
For all rejoiced to see this smile
Come from their sovereign lord.

The king, he graciously did sign
The paper that he saw,
And vowed that, for all time to come,
It should be British law.
The people cheered, and cheered again ;
The king, he laughed for glee,
For he was always well content
His people glad to see.
And now, when years have passed away,.
There still lives in our minds
The Magna Charta, with its laws
Of many different kinds.
And we still boast of liberty
Which it has brought about ;
So many privileges great,
We could not do without.
And still in feast and revel,
With shouting and with wine,
We sing of the great Charta,
Which good King John did sign.

(I was never myself at a dinner-party where they sang songs about the Magna Charta, but still—to conclude) :

And still we tell our children
The story handed down,
How this great deed was signed of yore,
In famous London town.

Worthy of Macaulay, that last bit; nevertheless I had some idea that the Magna Charta was *not* signed in the metropolis, but I suppose I must have been mistaken.

CHAPTER IV.

RUNNING EXPERIENCES.

"' Ho ho ! ha ha ! Tra la la la !
So sound the fairy voices.
From all the lowland western lea,
The Uxbridge flats and meadows,
From where the Ruislip waters see
The Oxhey lights and shadows;
From Wembley rise and Kenton stream,
From Preston farm and hollow,
Where Lyon * dreamed, and saw in dream
His race of sons to follow ;
They tell of rambles near and far,
By hedge, and brook, and border."

SCHOOL SONG.

MUST ask my readers to suppose a year to have elapsed since the events recorded in the last chapter. It is again Easter term; "torpids" are over, and running is in full force. Our hero is now an individual of some importance, having got his " fez," and being in the Upper Remove. He is in a room with a fellow called Lyon, who is in the Upper Shell—a pleasant companion when you once know him, but

---

* John Lyon, the founder of Harrow School, lived at a hamlet called Preston, a few miles from Harrow.

always very quiet, and certainly not a brilliant con-
versationist. At work he is not very bright, but he
is a good cricketer, and fair player at football. His
great strength lies in running, and of nothing is he
fonder than a good trot over the country on a half-
holiday afternoon; not one of your little runs a mile
down the Pinner road and back, or over to Kenton,
but a regular steady grind over to Elstree or Ealing.
Not that he is above an afternoon at Kenton Brook
now and then, but that is not his idea of a run.
Naturally Russell is most frequently his companion.
Lyon never runs out with more than two others.
Those big parties usually do more humbugging than
running. When he can get no one to come with
him, he starts off alone; but most often he is with
Russell, who has fallen into his paces, and the two
are a very good pair. One or two of their runs may
prove interesting to the reader.

It was a cold dull day in the beginning of March,
when Russell and Lyon sauntered up town after
breakfast. They strolled up to the school gates to
read the notices. One was to the effect that Mr.
—— and Mr. —— (farmers over Kenton way) had
consented to fellows running over their ground so
long as they did not smash the fences. It was all
very well, but how was anybody to know which was
Farmer Brown's, and which was Farmer Smith's?
So remarked Lyon on reading the notice. "Oh, it's
no odds," replied Russell, "if we do get on somebody's land who hasn't given his consent, we can but
say we didn't know."

That afternoon, after two bill, they started off
together over the Footer-field, past the back of
Ducker, and away across the fields to the railway,

then over the level-crossing, and across more fields
to "the Brook"—a run known to most Harrovians.
The floods had been out, and the water was unjump-
able, so they waded across by a dam, more than
knee deep, and proceeded up the hill which overlooks
the Kingsbury race-course. Then away over more
fields, until at last they lost their bearings, and
began to wonder how they should find their way
back again. "What's the time?" asked Lyon of
Russell, who carried the watch. "Twenty to four,"
he replied. "Oh, we'll never be back to four bill;
let's cut it, and go a long run." Accordingly they
ran on, until at last they came out on a road which
landed them at Hendon. Here they got some slight
refreshment, and prepared to return by the road.
However, when they reached Kingsbury, they thought
they would try a short cut home over the race-course,
and accordingly started in that direction. Before
they had gone very far they heard a shout, and
looking behind, saw a man a few fields off, signalling
to them. It was too late to stop and explain, besides,
he appeared savage, so they increased their pace—
the man after them; they expecting that he would
soon give in. Not a bit of it; the rustic seemed
determined to nail them. On they went, hiding
their caps to prevent his seeing what house they
belonged to. At last they gained the railroad, and
resolved to skulk down behind the hedge along the
line, hoping their pursuer would cross it and get on
the wrong scent. So he did; but they had not got
far before a new difficulty presented itself in the
shape of three irate navvies, who wanted to know
why they were trespassing on the line. In a few
minutes they, too, were in full chase, nor did they

give in till Russell and Lyon were a good way down
the Kenton road. No sooner were they rid of these
pursuers, however, than they saw coming towards
them, evidently disgusted at his failure, returning
by the road, their former enemy, the rustic; who,
on seeing them, at once attempted to cut off their
retreat. However, by a long roundabout way over
the fields in the direction of the station, they eluded
him, but he was not slow to follow them up the hill.
Lock-up bell was ringing as they went through the
town, and everybody stared to see two fellows at
such a time in running-clothes. They had to go in
to answer their names at "lock-up" without changing, but, thanks to long Ulsters, their garb was not
detected; and they afterwards had the satisfaction
of seeing their baffled pursuer, from their window,
telling his story to a group of "chaws," who seemed
vastly diverted at his expense.

A week or two after this adventure, Lyon got himself, Russell, and Burton "signed" for dinner and
two bill. It was a whole holiday, and they had resolved to run over to Uxbridge, where Lyon had some
friends, lunch there, and return in time for four bill.
Most fellows who heard of the plan were incredulous
—said it could not be done in the time, and so on.

However, nothing daunted, they started off immediately after eleven bill (having in fact previously
changed, and slipped on great coats and trousers
over their running clothes, for bill), and were soon
in full swing. They were not very clear about the
way, and the road they took was perhaps not the
shortest. After passing the top of the cricket-field,
they kept along the Northolt road, till they came to
the turn on the right which leads into the straight

stretch known as the "Uxbridge Mile." Having
walked over the little piece of connecting road, they
were able to do the mile at racing speed, Lyon being
first by a little, and Russell second, Burton having
given up a little more than half way. The two
others rather regretted having asked Burton to join
them, as he seemed likely to be somewhat a drag.
However, on the whole, he kept up pretty well till
they reached Ickenham, where he seemed very grate-
ful for a lift in a countryman's cart, which was
going into Uxbridge. The others kept up with the
cart most of the way. The party reached their des-
tination at a quarter to one, and after washing off
the dust of their journey, appeared at lunch. They
must have looked strange sitting down in such a
garb with ladies, in a civilised room ; but nothing
else could be expected, and their entertainers seemed
rather to enjoy the novelty than otherwise. Lyon
was very abstemious, for fear of not being able to
run afterwards ; but the unwary Burton was be-
guiled into making rather a hearty meal, and did not
refuse cake, the result of which imprudence was that
he was not in the best form on the return journey.
Not so very far from home, somewhere in the region
of the Rifle Butts, he complained that he was dead
beat ; the others said they would walk the rest of
the way with him, but he would not hear of it ; and
as Lyon was especially anxious to convince certain
unbelievers by turning up at four bill, they yielded
to Burton's wishes without much pressing, he saying
that he would follow quietly. As they reached the
foot of the hill the bell was ringing, but they managed to be just in time for bill, and afterwards
returned to the house to enjoy a bath after their ex-

ertions. This done, and some time having been spent over the fire, telling their adventures to a few idlers who came into the room, lock-up bell began to ring, and (the next day being Sunday) they hastened out to lay in provisions.

About seven o'clock, as Russell and Lyon were sitting over their exercises, in came " Jimmy " Belfield. " I say, didn't Burton start with you fellows out running to-day ? " he asked. " Yes," replied Russell, " but he got rather pumped, so we left him on the way home to follow at his leisure. Why do you ask ? " " Because the old man is in his study wanting to know why he didn't come to lock-up." " Didn't he ? " said Russell in surprise ; " why, I made sure he'd turn up all right ; but I'll go and have a jaw with the old man about it." So saying, he left the room, and was soon in the study telling all he knew of the matter to Mr. Kingsford. " Where did you leave him ? " asked the master. " On the road, just near the Butts," replied Russell. " Well, something must have happened ; he is a steady sort of fellow ; not likely to absent himself like this on purpose. Perhaps he has sprained his ankle, or got into a bog, or something." So saying, he rang the bell, ordered his carriage, and telling Russell to get ready to accompany him, went to prepare a lantern and get on his hat and coat.

Before very long the carriage was on its way along the road, the coachman keeping a sharp look-out on the sides of the road illuminated by the carriage lamps. When they got near to the spot where Russell said they had left Burton, they alighted, and with the aid of a big lantern investigated every likely place, expecting every moment to come upon a

huddled mass of humanity, or to hear a moan proceeding from the ditch. No; nothing met the eye
or ear. A cottage was near at hand, but all inquiries there were fruitless; nothing had been heard
or seen of the missing Burton.

After a long search they returned, giving up all
hope of making any discovery till the morning. It
was nearly ten o'clock by the time they pulled up
before the house. The door was opened by Crabbe,
the butler, who said, "Mr. Burton's all right home,
sir; he came back not very long after you left."

Burton was soon in the study, giving an account
of his misfortunes to Mr. Kingsford and Russell. He
had told his story already to most of the fellows in
the house, who naturally had been in some excitement before his return.

"After you left me," he began, turning to Russell,
"I went on all right, at a walk, for some little way.
However, before very long, a blister on my heel,
which I had felt slightly for some time, became so
much worse that I could hardly get along. At last
I had to sit down by the roadside to rest. Then I
went on for a bit, but soon I had to stop again, and
so on; so that it was pretty dark by the time I got
on to the Northolt road. Just then there came by
a great lumbering covered cart, which I hailed,
and asked the fellow who was driving if he could
give me a lift to Harrow. He said, 'Yes;' but
added that there was no place where I could sit
comfortably except on some sacks in the back part
of the cart. There it was quite dark, so that I could
not see whereabouts we were. However, I was well
content to get a place to rest myself; and in spite of
the jolting of the cart, I managed by some ill luck

to fall asleep; I suppose I was rather tired. The next thing I remember is being woke up by a gruff voice saying, close to me, 'Hullo, master! bless'd if I didn't forget all about you!' I started up, and saw it was the driver speaking. 'Where are we?' I asked. 'Why, down at 'Arrer station,' he replied. I must have slept long and soundly, for it seems that he went up the hill, and stopped at the 'Crown and Anchor' to get a drink (which probably in part accounted for his forgetting me); then he called at a shop where he had to leave a parcel, and then drove on down past 'The Grove' to the station. I got out, rubbing my eyes, and began to wonder how to get home. Walking was out of the question, as my foot was very painful. I managed, however, to get a fly (by the way, the man charged seven shillings and sixpence), and here I am safe at last."

This was the last time Burton tried a long run. "You see, it's not in my line," he would say.

That year Russell's house had a "mile," the cup being given by an old Harrovian. Owing to his success in the "half-mile" the year before, our hero's handicap was not very liberal; but, nevertheless, he would have managed to get a place at least, had not a vexatious accident occurred. Just as he turned the corner, and was beginning his "spurt," out rushed a big dog from among the bystanders, barking and careering about the road. By some evil chance he managed to get in front of the runner's legs, and down came Russell, cutting his hands badly and grazing his knee. This spoilt a very good race, as he, with Belfield and Lyon, were running neck and neck. As it was, the two others made a "dead heat" of it.

CHAPTER V.

CONCERNING WORK.

"Jack's a scholar, as all men say,
    Dreams in Latin and Greek,
Gobbles a grammar in half a day,
    And a lexicon once a week.
Three examiners came to Jack,
    'Tell us all you know ; '
But when he began, 'To Oxford back,'
    They murmured, 'we will go!'"
                            SCHOOL SONG.

AFTER the preceding chapter on athletics, it may be well, for a change, to turn to graver matters. Our hero, though he kept his place in form with no great difficulty, was never the ideal "master's boy," who goes into raptures over a Greek chorus, writes home to his people in Latin, and spends his half-holidays in reading Herodotus for his own amusement, or writing "Jambics" for the week after next.

Russell was of opinion that school-work was a necessity, very often an unpleasant one, but still a necessity that must be put up with. He didn't *mind* Homer and Virgil, but (nor was he singular in this respect) he could never be brought to see the beauty of such characters as Ulysses and Æneas, who always burst into tears on the very slightest provocation, and who, when asked who they are, reply, in a loud voice, " I am Ulysses (or Æneas, as the case may be, for one character seems cribbed from the other), renowned throughout the whole world, whose fame reaches the heavens!" or in modest words to that effect.

As to a Greek chorus, Russell hated the sight of one ; so that when an enthusiastic master would read out some passage with pathos or fervour, and exclaim, " Oh, it is *bee-yewtiful, bee-yewtiful*, isn't it ?" the unclassical Russell would smile, and make a remark to his neighbour which I shall not repeat.

Then again he failed to see any loveliness in a "prop." of Euclid, or a long sum in decimals, and he wondered why every "prop." could not be taken for granted, like the postulates, and what possessed the idiot who ordained that

$$5\tfrac{1}{2} \text{ yds.} = 1 \text{ pole}$$
$$2\tfrac{1}{4} \text{ inches} = 1 \text{ nail}$$

to introduce the fractions, unless it were to complicate sums and make fellows lose their temper.

Modern languages he saw more fun in. As to the exercises in French, he usually stuck anything down that came into his head, and then said, "Oh, of course !" in a tone of vexation, as each mistake was pointed out. As to the translations from French into English, I am afraid they were rather literal, and showed but few traces of the dictionary's use whenever a " shot " at the meaning of a word would do instead. As, for instance :—

" Mr. Crow, over a tree perched, held in his beak a cheese. Mr. Reynard by the odour disgusted, to

him a tint to a little near this language : ' Hi ! good
day, Mr. of the crow ! That you are jolly, that you
resemble a fine (man). Without mentioning it, if
your rummage reports itself to your plumage, you
are the phœnix of these hostile woods."

I refrain from copying more from Russell's exercise, but the above will show the talent and labour
expended on this part of his work.

Essays he revelled in, " because," as he would
say, "you can write such glorious bosh ! " To fill
sixty or a hundred and twenty lines of exercise paper
was his chief ambition, and that done, what remained on a Saturday night but to take his pleasure ?
This last usually consisted in roasting chestnuts in a
neighbour's room, or, better still, in getting up a
concert of combs, or a game of " high-cockalorum "
in the passages.

Co-operation, and assistance from the Cyclopædia
were freely resorted to in the production of essays.
As, for example, on the subject of "Astronomy;" the
Cyclopædia would be bagged from the house-library
early in the evening, and, at seven or eight o'clock
the essayists in the same form would appear in the
room of one of their number. Biscuits would be
produced, and the one who had, the Cyclopædia
would read out, " Astronomy is the science which
treats of the heavenly bodies, their motions, positions,
and changes," and then add, " that'll do for ten
lines at least." Accordingly a busy scratching of
pens for a few minutes, each one spreading out the
idea into as many words as possible, something in
this style : " Astronomy may be defined as a science
rather than as an art, and treats, for the most part,
of the stars which are distributed in such countless

numbers over the surface of the great canopy of sky
which covers the earth on which we live. Astronomy
teaches us much concerning the movements of these
heavenly bodies, and also of the varied and wonderful positions which Nature has destined them to
occupy ; moreover, it is by the science of astronomy
that we learn the changes to which these heavenly
bodies are subject." Then another piece would be
read and similarly expanded, and so on, till the
article in the Cyclopædia became too deep for the
ordinary mind. Then recourse would be had to
invention. "Oh, say something about a fellow with
a telescope! " suggests somebody. Whereupon, down
goes the idea, in this form, perhaps : "And so it is
that many a pleasant and instructive hour may be
spent with a telescope. By applying the eye to one
end of a tube, the wonders of the stars are revealed
to the man with the telescope. This is indeed a
wonderful thought, and one which ere now has
caused master-minds to stagger. To reflect that by
means of the telescope may be seen " (here the
writer seems to be at a loss for particulars, as he
goes on to say) " many wonderful things which
could not be seen with the naked eye—this is a
thought that few can thoroughly regard with calm-
ness." By this time the necessary number of lines
would be nearly filled up, and the essayist would
abruptly conclude with the following brief but mas-
terly peroration. " Astronomy, then, is the science
of the stars, and it is a very wonderful science, and
deserves encouragement. Long may it prosper!
(This last was encouraging, at least to the philoso-
pher.)

Latin prose bothered Russell terribly, and his

anger knew no bounds when one day, after finding a
piece in Cicero, and copying it out *verbatim*, he had
it returned full of corrections, and with the remark
that the style was "canine." Then again, masters
had such different ideas on the subject. His form
master would ·tell him always to put the *infinitive*
after "*negari non potest*," whereas such a proceeding
in his pupil-room prose would bring down the dis-
pleasure of his tutor, who declared that *quin followed
by subjunctive* was the correct thing. One day his
tutor said that it was convenient in many cases to
Latinise an English name; to put, for instance,
"Promontorium Septentrionale" for "North Fore-
land," and even occasionally "Faber" for "Mr.
Smith." However, when our hero next week dubbed
Francis Bacon "Lardum," his tutor didn't seem to
see it, which sadly puzzled poor Russell.

Then the "reps" were a source of trouble. Not
that he was positively unable to remember them,
but it cost him more trouble to do so than he usually
cared to expend. There are some fellows who can
read an ode of Horace through once or twice and
know it. There are others who cannot remember
two consecutive lines. "Odi profanum vulgus et
arceo," begins one of these unfortunates, then stops
dead. "Favete linguis," says the master, adding
"Why don't you think of the English?" Accordingly he does; "I, a priest of the Muses" he knows
it goes on, so he continues, "Ego sacerdos musarum."
"Does that scan?" asks the exasperated master.
Of course it does not, only he went by the English.
And so he "skews" his "rep" daily; goes after
dinner to the master's house; spends an hour, or
often two, saying it line by line; gets "puns" for

every mistake (as it is all counted for obstinacy);
and has to write out the English of every "rep"
through the term. Oh, and then the trial "rep!"
If it is old work, it is just like new *to him;* he
blunders, gets "skewed;" sent to "extra;" and
goes home for his holidays hours after every one else
has left, except a few martyrs like himself. If
masters would only reflect, they would surely cease
to imagine that any one would be such a fool as to
go through all these tortures out of sheer obstinacy.

Russell was *not* one of these hopeless cases, but he
"skewed" pretty often, and was frequently to be
seen in his form-master's study in the early part of
the afternoon. However, a quarter of an hour
usually saw him free.

Sometimes, after four bill, he would saunter into
the "Vaughan," to which he had a ticket, which he
rather regretted having paid for, as it was never once
demanded. He would peep into one book and
another, chiefly the illustrated editions of Scott's
novels and the poets. Then he delighted, for a
change, to lug out some huge volume, atlas or
Cyclopædia, and lay it on the superannuated chapel-
lectern, where he would stand to peruse it; this had
an air of importance, he thought. A great book,
with horrible coloured plates of the tortures of the
Inquisition, often occupied the lectern when he was
there. Occasionally, he would look over the bound
numbers of the "Harrovian," or the old "House-
lists." Once he got hold of the "Evidence before the
Commission on Public Schools," in the Harrow sec-
tion of which he saw it stated that "first school"
lasted only an hour, whereat he raved all the evening.

Altogether, he found a good deal to occupy his

attention in the " Vaughan," and came to the conclusion that it wasn't half a bad place to go to when
time hung heavy. The chairs were comfortable,
and the soft seat round the bay window was delightful. Besides, there were lots of things to see—the
racquet cup; the Ashburton shield (it was there
then); the old silver arrow and shooting costume;
the Wilkinson collection of antiquities and coins;
the Indian curiosities; the portraits of celebrities;
and no end of things besides; without mentioning
the books.

At work altogether, as a rule, he was not lazy;
that is, not lazier than many; and, as I have said
before, he managed to keep a respectable place in
form, and usually succeeded in obtaining a very fair
report, whereby his people were kept satisfied, for
they never expected him to turn out a genius; and
his father was well pleased to see that he did not
take to work to the exclusion of play, a proceeding he
had a horror of, having visions of brain-fever and the
south of France, as the results of a book-worm's
mode of life.

CHAPTER VI.

SUMMER TERM.

"If in the cricket-field sullen you've sat,
Doubting the value of ball and of bat,
Stray for a moment beneath the elm trees,
Nodding their heads to the tune of the breeze ;
Then, if you listen, their song you will hear
Rising in harmony measured and clear :
'This be your motto, ye sons of the hill,
Play with a purpose, and work with a will.'"

SONG OF THE HARROW CRICKET-FIELD ELM TREES.

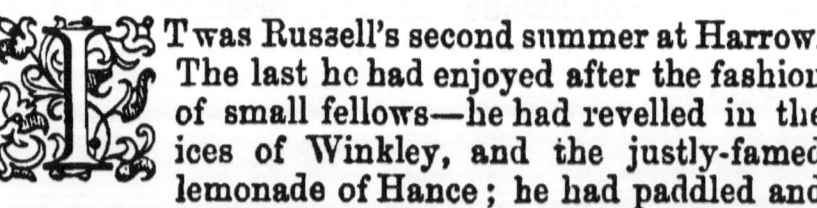

T was Russell's second summer at Harrow.
The last he had enjoyed after the fashion
of small fellows—he had revelled in the
ices of Winkley, and the justly-famed
lemonade of Hance ; he had paddled and
splashed in the shallow end of " Ducker ;" he had
lain on the grass in the cricket-field on match days,
consuming cherries by the hundred ; he had made
his *debut* at house games and in the school-yard ;
he had eaten voraciously on " Speecher ;" he had
shouted at Lord's till he was hoarse, and had trodden
on the toes of an irate old gentlemen (an old Etonian)
in his excitement ; he had, in short, done all that

was right, and proper, and pleasant, for a fellow
spending his first summer term at Harrow.

But this term he enjoyed himself even more than
last year; he knew more fellows, felt himself of more
importance, swam better, played cricket better, did
most things better, and felt more at home.

So, it may be imagined, he was supremely happy.
What more delightful than a whole holiday. The
delicious " froust;" nine bill; breakfast (perhaps up
at Winkley's—a luxurious and protracted meal);
eleven bill; "Ducker;" dinner; two bill; then the
whole afternoon down in the cricket-field, either
playing or watching the match; then six bill; and
then the cool evening to stroll up town, and sip
iced lemonade—was not all this the height of bliss?

Then Sundays in the summer term; the stroll
down to the fields before second chapel; the lying
there in the new-mown hay, under the shade of the
trees, when it was too sultry to go far; the walk
after evening chapel down the London Road, where
one seems to meet the whole school—these sunny
memories are sweet to many an old Harrovian,
strange as it may seem.

Russell was at this time a great enthusiast at the
"Gym." At first he had not liked it much, that is,
the regular routine, and was generally to be heard
answering his name from some remote beam in the
roof, where he would remain eating chocolate or some
other delicacy, till he was chased from his position.
However, he soon got to like the exercises, especially
the horizontal bar, round which he spun in a most
alarming manner, hanging by his eyelids, it seemed.

At "Ducker," too, he was singularly active; always
going off the running board, or the top place, or the

spring-board, or the bridge, or the top of a shed;
never in the same place two moments together,
always turning up where least expected. He had a
supreme contempt for the type of fellow who goes
down, languidly undresses, puts his finger in to see
if the water is cold, and then, after a long period of
irresolute shivering, crawls feet foremost down the
steps, splashes, gets out again, and then, swathed in
towels from head to foot, basks in the sun for half an
hour, never attempting to go in a second time.
Russell's plan of action was very different; he delighted in egg-diving, and swimming under water,
and all sorts of feats. He had a great dislike to the
practice of "ducking," and was only once known to
resort to it, namely, one day when he saw a great
bully of a fellow swim down, ducking every small
beginner he came to, whereupon our hero deliber-
ately swam up to him, laid hold of him by the
shoulders and dived, detaining him at the bottom,
till such time as the bully was on the point of drowning, when he released him, and went on his way as
if nothing had happened. Russell would probably
have won some swimming prizes that year, had he
not been taken ill before the end of the term.

Being free from cricket fagging, he had more time
to himself than the year before. At cricket he began
to distinguish himself, and was a leading member of
the "shell game." But his cricketing renown was
nipped in the bud that year. One day he found
himself in "Sicker," not feeling very well, and the
next in the "Sanny," with the scarlatina. He was,
unfortunately, the only patient there, and so was
not so merry as he might have been, had there happened to be any companions in trouble. However, he

managed to amuse himself—perused more novels
than he ever had before ; worked himself a pair of
slippers ; imbibed much lemonade, and altogether
was not overwhelmed with his misfortune. Still, it
was hard to be in bed when he knew that there was
some match going on in the cricket-field, or that the
festivities of " Speecher " were at their height ; and
his excitement on the day of the match at Lord's
was only equalled by his rage at being prevented
from being there. Telegrams, it is true, reached
him—about six each day—from various friends, but
they only increased his excitement.

Company, of course, during those weary weeks he
saw none, and his intercourse with the world was
confined to grins, through a closed window, at fellows
who came over to strawberries and tea in the
" Sanny" garden on Sunday afternoons.

The visit of the doctor was the great event of the
day, and to this was added, on Sundays, one from a
kind friend (one of the masters), whom every Harrovian knows and respects. Now and then a
rumour that another patient was coming to the
" Sanny" would form a little excitement ; but
these reports were never confirmed by the event.

At last, Russell was well enough to move about
the house, the mysteries of which were new to him.
The various rooms—the dining room, the doctors'
room, the disinfecting room, the sitting room, were
all explored, and in the last mentioned he was able
to spend a good part of each day. Then came preparations for departure, among which was the
custom of inscribing his name (and possibly something else) in the " book." He was asked to com-
pose some poetry to write in it, at which he demurred.

Others had written their names only, or copied something from Scott or Longfellow ; why should *he* do more ? However, after mature consideration, he resolved to try, at all events : it would be something to do. So he provided himself with a selection of steel pens and poetical epithets, a sheet of paper for the fair copy, and lots of foolscap for the rough, and began. No ; the ideas would not flow. Closeted for hours alone, or walking up and down from one place to another, the poet laboured, but with slow result. He grew quite pale under the mental pressure.

Tiddle-de | *tiddle-de* | *tum* ‖ *tiddle-tum-tum* | *tiddle-de* | *tum-tum.*‖

he would mutter desperately. Then, changing the metre—

Tit iddle | *tiddle* | *tiddle* | *tum* ‖ *ti-tiddle,* | *tiddle* | *ti.*‖

At last, patience and trouble were rewarded, and he one day laid on the table, with no little triumph the following lines—

> " 'Twas summer, and the little birds
> Were hopping on the trees ;
> The sultry atmosphere was full
> Of little flies and bees.
> The sun rose early in the East,
> And sank into the West,
> And we poor fellows sat in school,
> With ' phug ' and heat oppressed.
> And still the cruel master sat,
> In cap and gown arrayed,
> He would not let us doff our coats,
> However hard we prayed.
> It was not ' dignified,' he said,
> To sit without a coat ;
> We languid sat, too hot by far
> To write a single note.

4

I more than all (I know not why),
Felt the oppressive heat ;
I melted inch by inch, I'm sure,
While lolling in my seat.
O ruthless master ! why did he
Refuse so small a boon,
To sit in shirt-sleeves, in the hot
And broiling summer noon ?
At last, to aid me in my woe,
There came, one melting day,
One of those rummy things they have,
You know, in a Greek play—
I know the English of the phrase
Is 'god from a machine '—
'Some sort of lucky chance, you know) ;
I caught the ' *Scarlatine* !'
And now I live in realms of joy,
Where I can sit at case,
And wear my coat, or take it off,
Exactly as I please.
I drink the soothing lemonade ;
No work assails my head,
And I can spend much of my time
In ' frousting ' in my bed.
O 'Sanny,' in the future days,
When I am very hot,
And can't take off my coat in school,
And want a cooler spot,
And when with lessons sore beset,
And bothered is my brain,
O ' Sanny,' if I only can,
I'll turn up here again ! ''

The poem was rather lengthy ; but after trying in
vain to cut it down, the writer entered it, in his best
fist, in the " book ; " but his modesty prevented his
putting more than his initials after it.   About a
week afterwards he left the " Sanny," and went to
recruit his strength at the seaside, where we will
leave him, in the hope that he will be all right next
term, to begin his third year at Harrow.

CHAPTER VII.

COUSIN CHARLIE.

"Come o'er the stream, Charlie, dear Charlie, brave Charlie,
Come o'er the stream, Charlie, and dine wi' Mac Lean;
And though you be weary, we'll make your heart cheery,
And welcome our Charlie and his loyal train."

SCOTCH SONG.

"OMING down to see the match?" asked Russell of Acton, a fellow in another house. "Yes; are you? let's go down quietly, and we shan't be too soon." Two bill was just over, one day in footer term, when the above question and answer were exchanged. They went down accordingly past the New Schools, another fellow from Acton's house—FitzJames—joining them. "By the way," said Russell, "what was the row last night at your house? Devereux says you could be heard a mile off; he was at his window half the evening trying to make out what it was, and only heard a noise like a regiment of tipsy men, bawling and yelling like fury. He saw lights in your 'Pupe' windows, and the row seemed to come from there." "Oh, that was 'Chori,'" replied Acton; "don't you

know what 'Chori' is?" "Well, I've heard of it;
I don't think any house has it but yours. What's it
like?" "Oh, it's an awful lark; every one goes into
'Pupe,' and there's a table with a chair on it, put
for fellows to stand on. Then all the 'fezes' come
in with red dressing-gowns, and wearing their
'fezes.' They all sit down, facing the table, and
then the fun begins. They call out all the fellows
who have come into the house since last 'Chori,'
(it's only once a year, you know), and they come up,
one by one, and have to stand upon the chair that is
put on the table. Then the 'fezes' question the
fellow that's up about the footer rules, which he's
supposed to have learnt. There are two fellows in
house-shirts, one with a racket, and the other with a
toasting-fork, who lay into the unfortunate fellow
from below, whenever he makes a mistake." "But
what if he knows the rules perfectly?" suggested
Russell. "Oh, it's no odds; they ask humbugging
questions: 'What's the fourth letter in the second
word of the third rule?' or, 'What's the last word
on the sheet of the rules?' Sometimes the fellow
has got up even that, and says at once the last word
in the *last rule;* but he's dodged there, because the
last thing *on the sheet* is the *printer's name!*" "It's
best fun," broke in FitzJames, "when they have a
great fat fellow up, or some big chap that's migrated
from a 'small house.'" "Yes, and then," continued
Acton, "after that, every one in the house, beginning
at the 'lag,' has to get up and sing a song, holding
a 'tolly,' standing upon the same chair, on the
table. Some fellows can't sing a bit, but it's no
matter; they have either to yell out some song, or
chant a house-list, and nobody is such a muff as

to do the house-list." " Wasn't McFarlane's song good ? " said FitzJames. " Oh, yes, awfully; he wanted it to be awfully sentimental, and the fellows got tired, so they came in with a chorus of ' He's a jolly good fellow ! ' between each verse ; McFarlane was awfully savage ! " " Jackson's song was rattling good, too," said FitzJames ; " but then that was meant to be comic, and had a splendid chorus ; and ' God save the Queen ' was fit to bring the roof down. By Jove ! *didn't* we yell, just ? I should think Devereux heard *that*, and fellows in houses much further off than his."

By this time they had reached the ground. It was awfully muddy and slippery. Play had not begun, but the two elevens were seen coming down the hill, and there were a good many spectators already. It was the first house match that year, and was expected to be a close thing. Russell and his two companions were not personally interested, as their respective houses were neither of them going to play. At last the players were ready, and the ball was kicked off. The opposite side soon ran it down to their enemy's base, but met with no little resistance ; and an interesting match was just commencing, when Russell heard a voice, and turning, saw a Fourth-form boy from his house, who breathlessly informed him that there was some one waiting to see him up at the house. " Who is it ? " inquired Russell. " I don't know; but I was just coming down, when Bardale told me to look sharp down, and find you, and say you were wanted."

It was provoking, after our hero had just come down, and it was going to be such a good match too. However, he couldn't help it, so he started off up

the hill. How he wished, as he plodded up through
the mud, that there were a tramway or something ;
but it was no good thinking of impossibilities. When
he arrived in his room, he found his " frouster "
occupied by a stout party reading the paper. His
back was turned to him as he entered, but as soon
as he heard a step, the gentleman rose with a bounce,
and proceeded to shake hands cordially, wringing
Russell's hand nearly to a pulp in his vehemence.
He was a youngish man with dark whiskers and a
large moustache. As I have said, he was inclined
to corpulence ; and he was dressed in the height of
the fashion. "Ah! so glad to see you, old man ;
hope you're quite well." (Russell hadn't a notion
who he was.) "Don't suppose you know me," he
continued, "as we've never met. Your cousin
Charlie, I am ; ha, ha ! thought I'd run down from
town and look you up. Hope your family are quite
well. I don't know much of them ; I'm only a
fourth cousin, you see !" Russell had heard of a
cousin Charlie, but he never thought he was a fellow
like this. *His* cousin Charlie, he had always under-
stood, was such a quiet sort of cove, not at all like the
flashy individual before him. He began to think he
was a swindler, and looked round the room to see
if anything was missing ; not that it would have
been worth any one's while to steal any of his books
or ornaments. He could but be polite ; still, he
must be on his guard.

"Let's come down and see the football, eh ?"
continued Charlie, slapping him violently on the
back. Russell followed the stranger diffidently,
taking the opportunity of being behind, to see that
his watch and money were all safe. The fellow had

a very loud voice, as well as appearance. Six years
in Australia had not improved his manners. As they
neared the footer field, lots of fellows stared, and
looked as if they were making remarks. Russell
wished himself well out of it. To be seen walking
with a great fat fellow, dressed in "three-man-
checks," with enough jewellery for six, smoking a
cigar, and talking, every now and then, loud enough
to be heard at Pinner—this was altogether most
unpleasant. Still he could not shake him off, and
if it were really his cousin, it wouldn't do to be rude.
" Aw, I was here years ago, don't ye know? Place
altered wonderfully; hardly knew it, except for the
Old Schools, and a few other places." Everybody
could hear all he said, and Russell felt that he
and his companion were objects of universal attention. " Aw, by Jupitaw! *that* was a good bit of
play? I remember a fellow in my day, who used to
' sky' every man in the field, like so many nine-
pins, and then do just what he liked with the ball !"
With such remarks the stranger passed away the
time until the footer bell sounded, when every one
began to make their way up the hill.

As fellows passed, Russell felt that Charlie was
being narrowly scrutinised, and his feeling of
awkwardness did not diminish when, on reaching
the house, they had to elbow their way through a lot
of fellows in the passages, who stared, open-mouthed,
at the stranger. Once in his room, our hero began
to feel more at ease; but soon Lyon (his room-
fellow) sloped in, quite unconscious that a visitor
was present, with a " tosh" full of water, in
" footer" clothes. "Oh, er—this is a—a cousin
of mine, who has—er—come to see me," stammered

Russell, hoping Lyon would either postpone his
ablutions or perform them elsewhere. But Lyon
was much too dense to take the hint, and, after
giving a sort of awkward bow in Charlie's direction,
proceeded to divest himself of his muddy garments,
utterly regardless of Russell's imploring glances.
" Well," said he at last, in despair, " shall we come
up to the school-yard ? It's nearly time for bill."
" All right," said his guest,—" must see old Sam,
don't ye know ? Wonder if he remembers me ? "
So saying, he swaggered down the passage, followed
by Russell.

" If Sam remembers him, he can't be a swindler,"
thought he, more puzzled than ever. Oh dear, yes,
Sam remembered him ; that is, when he gave his
name, which, by the way, did not sound like that of
Russell's cousin Charlie. Our hero was about to
take the bull by the horns, and ask his visitor if
there wasn't some mistake ; but bill was just beginning, and he didn't want to have a scene, as the
stranger was talking loud enough already.

During bill, Charlie distinguished himself by swaggering up and down in the open space in the middle,
until the bill-master, after eyeing him savagely for
some time, sent the monitor to ask him kindly to
retire, whereat he strode out of the yard in a rage,
muttering angrily. Of course this episode took
place before the whole school, and Russell felt more
ashamed of him than ever, and determined to avoid
him if possible. Accordingly, he watched him down
the street, and then turned into Davies' to get his
hair cut. After this he was at a loss where to go ;
he could not go to the house, for the awful Charlie
might be in his room, and he dared not go into

the school-yard or anywhere for fear of meeting
him.

At last, after cautiously looking up and down the
street, he ventured to Winkley's, and ordered muffins
and chocolate. The shop was crowded, and it was
some time before he got what he had ordered; but
at last it came, and being lucky enough to secure a
chair, he was just going to enjoy it, when the door
was opened, and in swaggered Charlie. Of course
every one looked up, and several might be seen whis-
pering that that was the fellow that made such a
row up at bill. "Aw—give me some chocolate,
will you?" he said. Russell was just behind him,
and was debating whether he ought to show himself,
or whether he could slip out unobserved, when the
difficulty was solved by Charlie, who, catching sight
of him, exclaimed, "Oh, here you are, you young dog!
Where have you been? I couldn't find you anywhere!
Wasn't that impertinence of that fellow to order me
off, up in the school-yard? Aw—I'd a good mind to
punch his head for him, the insolent hound!"
Russell felt ready to sink into the ground; of course
every one was listening, as they couldn't help it.
"Aw—let's come upstairs; nobody in the room, is
there?" So saying, he walked up, Russell following.

"Now then," said he, as soon as they had reached
the room, "just cut out, and bring in a few of your
friends, and I'll stand you all a regular high tea!"
Russell couldn't refuse, of course, so he went downstairs. Who should he ask? He couldn't introduce
So-and-so, because he'd get so unmercifully chaffed
about his noisy visitor. Lyon might do; he was so
dense, he'd never see anything to laugh at in the

whole affair. But then he'd been such a fool, beginning his "tosh," when the stranger was in the
room. Never mind; perhaps he wouldn't be recognised. "Look here, come up to tea at Winkley's
with me and that cove you saw; look sharp!" said
he, entering his room, where Lyon was writing
"lines." "Oh, I can't be bothered; I've got 'puns'
by lock-up." "Oh, cut them; I'll do you some lines
some day; come on, there's a good chap!" "Oh,
well, I don't mind, once in a way," said Lyon, good
naturedly, preparing to come. "Now for another
fellow," thought Russell. He couldn't think of a
suitable one. So, in despair, he collared the first
Fourth-form boy he met, and said imperatively,
"Now then; you're coming out to tea with me; just
brush your hair and come; be sharp!"

The small boy was surprised and delighted; he
had never been taken so much notice of before, and
a good feed for nothing was not to be despised! So
he came very willingly, and soon afterwards Russell,
with his two recruits, was seated with Charlie, doing
justice to a sumptuous meal in Winkley's upper room.
There was no doubt as to the stranger's liberality—
fish, hot meat, eggs, cold meat, tea and coffee, pastry,
all put in an appearance; and the guests made up
for their dearth of conversation by feeding heartily.
Before they had finished, lock-up bell rang, and
bidding a hasty good-night to their host (who observed that he would see Russell next day), they departed, arriving at the house just as the door was
being shut.

That evening Russell pondered over the adventures
of the afternoon, but could make nothing of them.
There *must* be a mistake. He had dropped his sus-

picious view of the stranger. To be sure, he was a
regular brick to stand such a tea, but he wished he
were not quite such a remarkable character, and
didn't talk so awfully loud.

Next day was Sunday. At first chapel, coming in
late, with very creaky boots, and wading among the
" toppers," Charlie was to be seen swaggering up the
aisle. His personal charms were enhanced by a
frock coat and a gorgeous crimson tie, while he
carried a white top hat, and wore an eyeglass. (This
last ornament he had not worn on the preceding
day, so it must have been part and parcel of his
Sunday attire.) After service, coming down the
aisle, he caught sight of Russell, to whom he gave a
familiar nod, making our hero wish himself anywhere
but where he was.

Nothing more was seen of Charlie till about ten
o'clock, when he appeared in Russell's room and proposed a walk before second chapel. While they were
out, the conversation turned on home affairs.
" Let's see ; you must be about sixteen. Ah ! yes.
I remember, your poor brother was two years older."
Russell stopped dead, and looked him in the face.
" I never had a brother," he said ; " there must be
a mistake." " Mistake ! nonsense ; why you'll be
telling me next that your name isn't Bertie Russell,
I suppose ! " " My name is *Hugh* Russell," replied
he. " Why, then, aren't you the son of old John
Russell, of Dellinghurst ; and wasn't your mother
a Miss Grove ? " " No, I'm the only son of Mr.
Russell, the Q.C., of whom you may have heard."

The " Comedy of Errors " was soon cleared up.
Of course our hero was not Charlie's cousin. That
worthy produced a letter in which the John Russell

he had spoken of wrote, " Bertie is getting on well
at school; I am sure a public-school life is doing
him good. Perhaps if you are in town, you could
run down and see him; it is not far by rail." And
to this alone was traceable the whole series of mistakes. The impetuous Charlie, being a Harrow man
himself, never doubted that the public school near
London referred to, was the " ancient school on the
hill;" but now he thought it over, he fancied it
must be *Eton*; and, in fact, he had some recollection,
now he tried to remember, that Bertie Russell *was*
at Eton; and as there was no one of the name at
Harrow, besides our hero, he supposed it must be so.
On his arrival at Harrow, he had asked the first
fellow he met if he knew any one of the name of
Russell, and if so, where he boarded, and the result
we know.

Russell was long afterwards " chaffed" about his
pseudo-relative, and at house-singing a solo was
always demanded of him of " Come o'er the stream,
Charlie!"

CHAPTER VIII.

THE " EX."

" A glimpse of home, and then away,
Back to the round of work and play—
A happy dream that soon was fled—
Things that were done, and thought, and said:
Was it for *this* we sighed and strained,
Of which the memory scarce remained ?
Nay, say not so; those few short hours
Refreshed us, roused our flagging powers;
To duty we returned once more,
Still heartier, stronger, than before."

ANON.

FOURTH school on the Friday evening of the " Ex." All the bother of getting " Ex-letters " and " Ex-papers " was over; all the suspense, all the threats of stopped " Exes," all the hopes and fears dependent on the discretion (or what the fellows thought caprice) of masters, were at an end. Even the formal entry of the monitor, followed by the reading out the names of those whose papers were signed, had taken place, and nothing remained for the Ex-goers in Russell's form but to sit quiet till the clock struck. The master had hit on this

peculiarly tantalising way of making the time seem
longer. At the beginning of school, lots of questions
had been asked among the fellows. "I say; I've
been packing my bag, and cut the ' con ' dead ; d'you
think he'll stop my ' Ex ' if I skew it ?" asked one,
anxiously. "Is there any chance of his letting us
out early ? " inquired another, though he well knew
that masters are never so aggravatingly punctual as
at the school before the " Ex."

At last the master came up, and soon every one
was in his place. One after another had been "put
on ;" nobody "skewed;" and they got through the
lesson before the hour was over.

Glances were exchanged, clearly denoting a hope
of an early release. Not a bit of it. The master
sat still, took out his watch ; ten minutes more.
Fellows grabbed at their hats and books, and sat on
the very edges of the forms, like cats about to
spring. Then the master gave out in a provokingly
deliberate way, the small amount of work expected
in the " Ex " from those who were not going. How
uninteresting it seemed to the anxious Ex-goers !
Somebody thought he heard the clock strike, and
accordingly stirred, whereupon half a dozen fellows
made a stampede for the door, one sprawling in the
middle of the floor in his anxiety to depart. But
they had to return to their seats, looking foolish
enough. " Four minutes and a half," quoth the
master," killing an animal which had crept from his
book. Then he began to mend a pen ; after which
he again consulted his watch, announcing that in
" three minutes and a quarter " they might go.

Russell was among the happy " signed," and was
to spend the " Ex " with Lyon, in London, his own

people being out of town. He had had several narrow
shaves of having his "Ex" stopped by various
masters, who had seemed to take a peculiar delight
in holding out this threat; so much so that our
hero had been provoked on one occasion, after the
oft-repeated threat had been brought out, to observe
that the joke was a trifle stale, which piece of impertinence nearly cost him his "Ex." But, as I
have said, suspense was now at an end, and at
length the wished-for moment arrived, and a second
rush was made to the door (that is by the Ex-goers,
the others taking it more leisurely). It was a foggy
November evening as Russell and Lyon, bags in
hand, sped down the hill. Many were the invitations from passers-by to take a place in a fly (already
containing five fellows, and two on the box), but
they heeded not. On they ran, passing and being
passed by other foot passengers. It was very dark,
and once Lyon ran head first into a ditch, where he
lay sprawling till pulled out by the legs by Russell;
other fellows were much too hurried to stop and
assist. Luckily, the ditch was comparatively dry,
so a small portion of mud, a battered hat, and a
torn umbrella, were the sole results of the fall. At
last the station was reached, and after the usual
bustle for tickets, the two found themselves on the
crowded platform. In a few moments the train
came up, and a rush was made. Russell and Lyon
were fortunate enough to get places in a first-class
carriage, and by the light of its lamp Lyon brushed
his garments which had suffered in the ditch.
Willesden was soon reached, and here they got out
and went up the stairs to the upper station, where a
quarter of an hour was spent in reading the advertisements.

When the train came up, it was no easy thing to find a place. It seemed to be full of people returning from their day's work. Trains do not wait long on the Metropolitan lines, so the two had hardly got into a third-class carriage before they were off. *Sitting* room there was none, as the occupants already consisted of four labourers, three volunteers, a snuffy old gentleman, evidently of Jewish extraction, with his son (a youth of unwashed appearance), and an old lady, who was the very ideal of Mrs. Gamp, umbrella and all. Lyon declined with thanks this kind old lady's offer of a seat on her knees; while Russell, with equal firmness and politeness, resented the efforts of the Jewish gentleman to make a place into which he might squeeze between him and his hopeful son. So they stood up, one at each window, trying to catch a little fresh air, as the atmosphere of the compartment was close, to say the least of it. At last the train stopped suddenly, sending Russell into the arms of one of the labourers, who received him with a volley of the abuse for which the British workman is so justly famed, while Lyon was soon receiving a hardly more polite reprimand from the old Jew, on whose toe the sudden stoppage of the train had caused him to tread. But all troubles have an end, and before many minutes had passed, the two found themselves driving in a hansom through the streets of South Kensington.

At length they pulled up before Sir Walter Lyon's house. The family were dining out, so the two were left to their own devices. After a solemn dinner, the solemnity of which was increased by the presence of the solemn butler, the two young bachelors sallied forth in a hansom to the Gaiety Theatre, where they found a capital farce, and met several of their schoolfellows. On their return home, Russell was introduced to his host and hostess, their eldest son, Harry, and their two daughters, grown-up young ladies.

Next day, after breakfast, the two friends set out in search of amusement; and, after doing some of the South Kensington Museum, and some shopping, went to lunch at the Criterion, from whence they made their way to the Christy Minstrels' afternoon performance. It was some time since either of them had witnessed the ever new and varied extravagances of this company, and for weeks afterwards their room at Harrow would resound, while they were dressing, with choice duets they had picked up at the St. James's Hall. The jokes too, and the farce at the end, were as good as ever, and Russell acquired the art of alighting sittingwise on a chair, with his legs rigidly stuck together up in the air, and his name not seldom appeared in the "breakage-list" for the remainder of the term in consequence. They returned home for dinner, after which they went off together, in company with Harry Lyon, to see "Our Boys." They had a box to themselves, from whence they got a good view of the stage and audience. Among the latter, Russell saw no less a person than "cousin Charlie;" and what was more, Charlie saw him, and made frantic efforts to catch his eye. At last, between the acts, Charlie was seen to leave his seat, and soon the door of their box opened, and a well-known voice was heard, saying, "Hullo, youngster, how are you?" and, taking possession of the remaining

chair, Charlie sat down, and stayed till the end of
the piece. He had found out his *real* cousin at
Eton, he said, and thought him a slow young ass,
and wished he'd stuck to his first-found relative.
This he seemed fully determined to do now at any
rate, and would only reluctantly take an excuse from
Russell for not coming to supper with him at his
club. However, they managed to shake him off at
last, and returned home.

Next day was Sunday, which was spent in the
morning by going to church, and in the afternoon
by visiting the Zoo.

Monday morning saw the two once more at
Harrow, racing up the hill, late for second school.
They had to get their books, and change their coats,
and, on reaching their room, they found most of the
former had disappeared. This, they subsequently
discovered, was caused by a black-mail, levied by
the fellows in the house who had not gone for their
" Ex," and who, to while away the time, had
extemporised a billiard-table and its appliances
out of an ordinary table, with books for cushions,
and umbrellas for cues. Moreover, they had got up
a fancy-ball, whereby the wardrobe of the Ex-goers
had suffered—even their towels and curtains being
taken for apparel. So that Russell could neither
lay hands on his books nor on a pair of " tails," so
he had to go up late, and hot, with somebody else's
books (which were pounced on by the master), and
a coat nearly down to his heels, the property of a
tall neighbour. He vowed he would get locks put
to his clothes-press and book-cupboard, which he
did, but found the doors of both burst open a few
days afterwards, by some one in a hurry, he supposed.

He was not such a sufferer as some of his neighbours, however, one of whom had returned from his "Ex" to find all his ornaments smashed, and two pictures with the glasses cracked; an occurrence accounted for by the fact that his open door had been made one of the bases of a spirited game of "passage-footer."

CHAPTER IX.

COCK-HOUSE MATCH.

" Routs and discomfitures, rushes and rallies,
Bases attempted, and rescued, and won,
Strife without anger, and art without malice—
How will it seem to you forty years on?
Then, you will say, not a feverish minute
Strained the weak heart and the wavering knee,
Never the battle raged hottest but in it,
Neither the last nor the faintest were we!
Follow up! Follow up!! Follow up!!!
Till the field ring again and again,
With the tramp of the twenty-two men,
Follow up! Follow up!! "

HARROW FOOTBALL SONG.

DULL morning, made still more dull by a persistent drizzle, which threatened ruin to any new "straw" which its owner was incautious enough to take out for its first airing.

The weather showed no sign of clearing, and Russell stood at the house door meditating. Cock-house match was to be played that afternoon, and his house was one of the rivals. He did not feel in particularly good "form," and was a trifle despondent

on the subject; perhaps the weather had something
to do with his melancholy frame of mind.

It will be remembered that he had got his "fez"
the year before, so a house match was a familiar
thing to him. But a *cock-house match*—that meant
something more. If only he felt up to it, what
wonders he would do; but somehow it seemed that
his wind, his running, and his powers altogether
had been declining the last few days. So at least,
in his present state of mind, he fancied; for no one
had found fault with his play of late. By and by
Lyon came out, on his way up town, and Russell,
discovering that he had borrowed his umbrella, had
to remonstrate, as he would soon want it himself.
This little event turned the train of our hero's
thoughts, and after he had seen Lyon off the
premises with an umbrella other than his own, he
returned to his room to prepare his garments for the
great contest. He was not usually particular as to
his dress at "footer," but on such a great occasion
he felt it his duty to the house to present as smart
an appearance as possible; so he selected the most
spotless pair of duck-knickerbockers, and the least
faded house-shirt, after which he took down his
"house-match fez" from its peg of honour over the
mantelpiece (he had three, one for house matches,
another for ordinary use, and a third for wet
weather), brushed it carefully, and combed its silken
tassel. Then he took out a woollen comforter of
house colours, to "go down" in, and a "fez-belt,"
and next proceeded to see to the stockings and
boots. After all his preparations were finished, he
went "up town" to gather intelligence of the
enemy's forces.

At dinner he eat of the beefsteak, which the fore-
thought of the matron had provided, and of course
abstained from pudding.   After the meal he repaired to his room, where he beat up an egg he
had previously procured, with hot water and a
little sherry that had been in his travelling flask
since the holidays.

This strength-giving mixture he drank out of his
tooth-glass, and gave some to Lyon, who pronounced
it " beastly," but, nevertheless, seemed to place unlimited faith in its powers.

After bill they " changed " as quickly as possible, and marched down to the field in proces-
sion, headed by " Jimmy " Belfield, who was captain
of the " footer," as well as cricket that year, and
whose popularity was greater than ever.   Amongst
the players whose names are known to the reader
were Burton, Leigh, and Vernon.   The last of these
had not got his " fez," but was first " choice," as
the list now stood.

The rain had ceased, but the ground was in a
fearfully slippery state.   Their opponents were on
the ground before them, and there was some discussion as to whether this was a good omen or not.
The whole school seemed to be on the ground, to
say nothing of masters, old Harrovians, and a fair
sprinkling of ladies.   Then there was the usual
knot of school-servants, tradesmen, and " chaws."
Altogether Russell, as he stripped, thought he had
never seen the ropes so crowded, and he felt on his
mettle. Play soon began, Russell's house (which, for
convenience, we shall call the " black and white ")
defending the base furthest from " Ducker."   The
wind was in their favour, and before long Burton

managed to run the ball between the enemy's poles.
The cheers were tremendous; one would have
thought that the shouts would never stop. But now
a harder task lay before the "black and white"
side. The wind right in their teeth, to which was
now added driving rain, made it no easy matter to
work the ball up to their opponents base, and after
a long and hard struggle, during which it was
difficult to say who were getting the best of it, so
exactly in the middle region did the ball keep, a
well-directed kick by the captain of the other side
made the state of affairs equal.

And it seemed as if the day's play would result in
a tie. Half-time passed, but still no more bases for
either side were kicked. The excitement grew
intense. Every "run-up," every fall, every catch,
was made the subject of deafening applause. The
ground was literally covered with lemons. "Ten
minutes more," shouted some bystander, "play up!"
"Five minutes only!" was soon the cry, and it
seemed as if it were too late for any decision of the
match that day. Some fellows, indeed, among the
onlookers, began to make their way up the hill,
thinking nothing more was to be seen. But they
were mistaken. A final effort was made by both
elevens; the play got faster than ever; not a laggard
was to be seen in the field.

In a lucky moment Russell took the ball from an
advancing foeman, and succeeded in making a
splendid "run-up," dodging one after another of his
opponents. He was well followed up, and when,
almost dead beat, he stumbled and fell, "Jimmy"
Belfield took the ball on till he was up again, when
he gave our hero a catch. The suspense was breath-

less. "Be quick; no time to lose!" cried somebody.
All depended on him. To "be quick" without
getting flurried, is no easy thing, especially when
the result of "cock-house match" depends on your
success or failure. A dead silence; every eye is
upon him. One quick glance, and he runs forward;
the ball soars in the air, and falls between and
behind the poles. Not a moment too soon. Before
the ball has stopped rolling, before every one has
realised what has happened, the bell begins, all doubt
is at an end, and Kingsford's is cock-house for the
year.

For a few moments our hero hardly realised the
feat he had performed, but he was soon roused to a
sense of it by the congratulations and praises that
poured in from all sides. As the players went up
the hill, too, he received sundry slaps on the back
from enthusiastic friends; and when they neared the
House, the scene of triumph came to its climax.
The street was full of fellows; the house door was
crowded; and as each player entered the house, he
was received with loud applause. When the fellows
caught sight of Russell, nothing would satisfy them
but to carry him into the house in triumph; nor did
they release him till they had landed him, clothes
and all, in a hot bath in his room, which they
had prepared for him. After his ablutions, the old
butler showed his loyalty by bringing him some hot
cocoa. After four he received company in his room,
sitting enthroned in his "frouster," which, rickety
at all times, succumbed under the weight of our
hero's newly-acquired honours, and let him down on
the carpet, in the midst of the Levée.

That evening a grand spread was given in the

Hall; speeches were made, and sherry-glasses broken.
Of course, Russell was *the* hero of the evening, though
many others of the players were " toasted." After
the spread, Russell was invited on to the " private
side," to be shown off and patted on the back by the
ladies, and this ordeal was the worst of any to him,
as he was never brilliant in company, and on this
particular evening he felt more than usually awkward, submitting to his pattings and compliments
with that air of resignation peculiar to small dogs
and school-boys who have done something out of the
ordinary. He was altogether glad to escape from
the drawing-room to his own humbler apartment,
which he found crowded with fellows, all talking at
once, the subject of conversation being, of course,
the house match. " Did you see ——'s run up ? "
" Who was it that got hurt, about half-time ; one of
the ——ites ? " " Wasn't that a good kick of Russell's ? " &c., &c.

Our hero's entrance was the signal for another
violent demonstration of approval, from which he
barely escaped with his life. On the whole, he was
not sorry, on a by-no-means-invented plea of fatigue,
to retire early to bed, with leave to " stop out " next
day from first school. He slept soundly—so soundly
that he did not even dream, as might be expected,
of the exciting scenes he had gone through during
the day. But next morning he awoke with a two-
fold consciousness of something pleasant: Firstly,
that his house was cock-house, and secondly, that he
was signed for first school. And with these sweet
reflections, he turned over to enjoy his well-won
" froust."

CHAPTER X.

"TRIALS."

"Some book-worms will sit, and will study
  Alone, with their dear selves alone,
Till their brain like a mill-pond grows muddy,
  And their heart is as cold as a stone.
But listen to what I now say, boys,
  Who know the fine art to unbend,
All labour, without any play, boys,
  Makes Jack a dull boy in the end."

OLD SONG.

RUSSELL was very anxious to secure his "remove," and, as his "quarter-marks" placed him in an uncertain position, he took to regular hard work for "trials." Never had he spent such a "trial-week." This period had usually been to him one of idle excitement, as he never did anything towards getting up his work, preferring to take his chance as the papers came, looking upon the whole as a sort of game of hazard, in which he was, as a rule, fairly successful. But this term it was altogether different. He was determined to get his "remove" at any cost. Accordingly, when the list of "trials" was read out,

he made a table of them, and stuck it up in his room
as a guide and reminder.

All his spare time on Sunday was occupied in reading up abstracts of Bible history, and making syste-
matic notes. Then he got all the commentaries he
could, and read through several hundred pages of
Stanley's " Jewish Church," and such works. His
labours were not nearly finished by bedtime, and he
determined to risk being " twug" in the act of
" tollying up." Luckily for him and Lyon (who
joined him in his preparation), Mr. K. did not come
round the house that night ; so the two sat on, hard
at work till about twelve, when, feeling sleepy, they
gave up the remainder of their good intentions, and
turned in.

Next day, seven o'clock (barbarous hour!) saw
them in school. It was quite dark, and the gas was
necessary almost till the end of school. Russell
came out feeling very fairly satisfied with his work,
but vexed that he should have had to miss several
questions that he might have done if he had prolonged his work the night before. He was determined it should not occur again. Accordingly,
before beginning " tollying-up " *that* night, he made
arrangements to defeat any inclination to sleep, with
tea and other things. After being nearly " twug "
twice, he continued his work in peace. At twelve
he again became sleepy, but swallowed some strong
tea, and walked about the room, to the annoyance of
the dozing Lyon. This had the desired effect, and
he returned to his books like a giant refreshed.
After he had been working for about an hour, his
" tolly " burnt itself out ; so he started off in the
dark with a match-box to forage for another. Groping

along the passage, the first door he came to was that
of Parkes, a Sixth-form fellow. After several inef-
fectual attempts to arouse the sleeping owner, Russell
bagged a " tolly " off the mantelpiece, and returned
to work. But his proceedings were soon stopped by
the " tolly " going suddenly out—a phenomenon
which was explained on the following morning by
the discovery that it was what Parkes called a
" decoy " candle, viz., one from which all the wick
had been carefully extracted, except half-an-inch or
so left at one end. " Teach fellows to come bagging
my ' tollies,' " remarked Parkes.

A second expedition was more successful, and
Russell did not give over work till two, when he had
promised to wake several fellows who preferred sleep
before work. First there was Burton. Never was
there such a fellow to sleep. Russell vowed that he
would never again undertake the waking of him.
He called him: no answer. He called again: only
a grunt. He shook him : two grunts. He pulled
the clothes off : a muttered expostulation. After
this had gone on for some minutes, our hero bethought him of water. Water he accordingly tried.
The abuse which followed was tremendous, but not
sufficient to arouse the sleeper, who, after sitting up
in bed, threatening to throw a boot at the intruder,
and using strong epithets, lay down again, and
composed himself to sleep. One more effort the
conscientious Russell made, but it was the last;
and he soon left the room, followed by a boot, a
brush, and the jug of water, which smashed against
the wall ; and as he retreated down the passage he
heard Burton snoring again, as if nothing had
happened.

The next two fellows were easier to wake, but the third was almost as difficult as Burton had been, only that he was not so active. He suffered himself to be pulled out of bed, and was at once fast asleep on the floor, where in the end Russell left him, having no more time to waste, as he wished to return to his room and commence his long postponed slumbers. In the morning, owing to his short sleep, he was so drowsy all first school that he could hardly do the paper ; and he resolved not to sit up again, but to try the early-rising dodge in future.

Next day there was Greek, and our hero thought he knew the " con " and parsing pretty well; but, strange to say, he had not a notion of the story of the books the form had read during the term. Accordingly he repaired to Penfield's room. Penfield was a clever fellow, in the Sixth form, who did everybody's work except his own, which he seemed to know by intuition ; a " rep" he read through once and knew, while " cons " he could do off at sight, as easily as he could read the newspaper.

As Russell entered his room, he found it occupied by about six fellows, big and little, all seeking help from the oracle. When he could get in a word, our hero addressed himself to Penfield, who sat in state in his "fronster." "Oh, I say ; just tell us the story of this Homer, will you ? I know the *con*, but if they ask the *plot*, I'm done for ! " " Oh, I really haven't time," replied the learned one, " I've promised to give Crawdon a 'con' of an Odyssey, and Leigh a ' con ' of some Horace, and then there are some fellows coming at ten to be put up to some dodges in algebra, and I've got to do a lot of 'jam-

bics' for Parbury, and a 'teek' exercise for Donald-
son, besides some trigonometry and a German 'con'
for Stoner, and as to my own trial-work, I've not
looked at it at all yet; no I really haven't got
time ! "

"Oh, *I'll* tell you the yarn of your Homer," exclaimed Crawdon; "come into my room, I know it
off beautifully; I'll be back in a few minutes, Penfield ! " he added, and the two left the den of learning
together. "Now then," said Crawdon, as soon as
they were seated over his fire, "Ninth Odyssey, isn't
it? Very well; open your book. You see, at the
beginning of the ninth book, Ulysses is sitting on
the hearthrug in Alcinous' best room. (You know
he has just had a fit of blubbering, and Alcinous
caught him at it, so he told the fiddler to hold his
row, because it seemed to bore Ulysses. All that is
preliminary. Well, then; now begins the ninth
book.) Ulysses begins his yarn; first, he says that
having a spread isn't half bad fun; then he says
that his name is Ulysses, and tells them that he is an
awful card, and no end of a nailer, and all that.
Then he starts his real story. He says that when
they left Troy they got among some coves called
Ciconians, whose town they sacked, but who afterwards gave them a drubbing. So they got into their
ships, and sailed off till they came to a rummy place
where there lived a set of fellows who did nothing but
eat buttercups. Some of Ulysses' men went on shore,
but they stayed there, eating buttercups too; so
Ulysses lugged them down into the boat, and pinned
them under the seats, and rowed off somewhere else.
The next place they came to was an island near the
place where Cyclops and his friends lived. Ulysses

and twelve of his fellows went to look about them,
and came to the cave where this monster lived.
(He was a big lout with one eye, you know. I think
he was called 'Polly-famous;' but don't bother
about that; just call him 'Cyclops.') Ulysses
'specked' on getting a hospitable present, but he
was sold there, for when the Cyclops came back,
after talking a little he ate up a brace of men, which
put the others rather in a funk. Next day, when
Cyclops woke up, he saw to his flocks, and then
thought he'd like some breakfast, so he took so to
speak, 'two of men, *without* * ' (without *mercy*, I suppose). Then he stuck a big stone in the door-way,
and went out. While he was out, that dodger
Ulysses hit upon a plan, so he got a big stick (he
says it was as big as the mast of a merchant-ship,
but that's all my eye, because he couldn't have lifted
it). Well, he and his fellows cut and burnt the stick
into a point, and hid it. When Cyclops came back,
he eat two more fellows, and then Ulysses gave him
some wine, which made him awfully drunk. While
he was asleep. Ulysses and his men made the stick
red-hot, and rammed it into the old man's eye. He
sang out, but it was no good; they gouged away at
his eye till it came out by the roots. After that,
some of the Cyclops-chaps came, and asked him what
was up, but he said, 'Oh, nothing at all!' (it's
some stupid pun in the Greek), so they chaffed him.
and went home. Next day, when old Cyclops drove
his cattle into the fields, he didn't know that Ulysses
and his fellows were hanging on underneath the
animals' stomachs, but that was their little game;
and the next that the old chap heard was Ulysses

* Vide Glossary.

chaffing him from the ship, for he had got on
board and bagged all the sheep. When Cyclops
heard that, he was awfully savage, so he got a stone
and whizzed it at the ship, nearly sinking it. Then
he tried to get Ulysses to come back, and said he'd
make it awfully jolly for him, and all that, but
Ulysses wasn't quite such a fool, so he gibed at the
old fellow again, who swore heavily, and buzzed
another stone at his head. Then they got back to
the other fellows, and had a spread ; and there the
book ends ! By Jove ! time for me to go up ! " So
saying he snatched up his blotting-pad, and rushed
out of the room, leaving our hero to commit to
memory the tale he had heard. Really though, it
did him good, for when he saw in the paper, " Give
a short sketch of the story narrated by Ulysses in Od.
IX.," he was able to put together a very creditable
answer.

Another help, too, he got from Crawdon, which,
however, turned out less successfully. Crawdon
did German ; Russell did French. Before the
"trial" in Modern Languages, the two exchanged
some knowledge. " Look here," said Crawdon, " if
you tell me some French, I'll tell you some German ;
and then we can both do some questions, besides
our own papers, and we'll score awfully ! " Accordingly Russell told Crawdon a few things likely
to appear in the French paper, and " conned "
some pieces to him, after which Crawdon said—
" Thanks ! now let me ' con ' you a bit of German.
I'll do the likeliest bit, one that we've been over a
dozen times. It is almost certain to be set. I have the
' con ' written out, and you can learn it like a ' rep ';
then, when you see the piece in the paper, you can just

set to, and write it out in English from memory!"
"But I don't know a word of German—I can't
even read all the letters," objected Russell. "Oh,
never mind; look here, the heading of the piece is
Der geheilte Hund, which means 'The cured dog.'
You will know if it is the same piece by the *Hund*
(think of *hound*), and then all you've got to do is to
write out the 'con' from memory." Accordingly,
Crawdon "conned" it through, and gave a written
"con" to his pupil, who learned it off like a "rep."
When he got into school, after he had finished the
French paper, he turned his attention to the German.
Sure enough, there was the magic word! (It was
spelt *Hunde*, but that did not matter, he thought.)
So down went the story of the "cured dog." He
was very much elated at his success, and made sure
that he would get a "copy" in Modern Languages.
He did not see Crawdon till after tea, when that
young gentleman at once began, "Oh, I'm awfully
sorry that German piece wasn't set! I made sure it
would be." "What? not set?" replied Russell in
astonishment, "it *was* set, and what is more, I did
it rattling well!" Then, and only then, it struck
him that there might be more than one piece of
German, in the heading of which the word *Hund*
occurred! The piece actually set was quite different
from the one he had translated; and next time
Modern Languages "Trial" came round, he did *not*
aspire to the German paper.

I have before said that our hero had renounced
sitting up to do "Trial" work, and had determined
to rise early instead. The first time he tried this,
the clock which he had borrowed failed to go off
at the required time, and Russell did not, therefore,

6

rise till the usual hour, and, in consequence, did a very feeble paper.

Next night, he borrowed a clock which was warranted never to fail. In order that it might make a sufficient noise, he placed it at the bottom of a basin, which he set on a chair by his bed. Sure enough, it went off at three (the hour at which he had set it), startling the sleeper, so that he gave his head a severe bang against the back of the bedstead. The clock did not cease warbling for about ten minutes; its internal commotion causing it, all the time, to walk about, and attempt to scale the sides of the basin. Once roused, our hero set to his work with a will, and had done several hundred lines of Virgil before he remembered that he had promised to wake some fellows. This done, he found it was time to join a " swotting-party," to which he had been invited. The hour fixed was 4.30 A.M. When Russell entered the room, he saw that most of the party had assembled. Besides the owners of the room, there were Burton, in a dressing gown of gorgeous pattern, Leigh, with a tail coat over his night-shirt, and Vernon, in a house-shirt and a pair of trousers (he said he always wore flannel next his skin in the early morning). The room looked out on the street. The birds were already singing, or rather, making a row. It is a peculiarity of the Harrow birds, that they are never heard or seen by day, but, whenever one is " tollying-up," these nocturnal creatures kick up the most awful row—not singing, but *shrieking* with all their might.

" Let's have something to warm us, before we begin swotting," said somebody. Accordingly, before long, thanks to an Etna and some mysterious tins,

they were all eating hare soup, steaming hot, out
of soap-dishes, tooth-glasses, and chimney ornaments. In the midst of the feast, there was heard
a strange noise outside, and on everybody rushing to
the window, they saw, by the light of a neighbouring
street lamp, a man—evidently the worse for liquor,
seated in a puddle in the middle of the road, addressing himself to anybody who cared to listen.
Finding he had an audience, he became more lo-
quacious; but before long "somno vinoque sepultus"
curled himself up on the pavement, and was soon
snoring loudly. So loudly did he make his sleeping condition known, that no one could attend to
their work. Some one suggested dousing him with
water, but, fearing he might become abusive, they
refrained. At last he rose, and staggered into the
porch, where he continued his sleep, terrifying the
maid who opened the door an hour later to clean
the steps. By the time that they had watched him
into the porch, the "swotting-party" found it was
about 5.30, and as no one felt inclined to work, after
a second brew of hare soup, they went off round the
house to torment their sleeping neighbours. The
amount of work done by our hero, at the "swotting-
party," was absolutely *nil*, nor were the others much
more industrious.

He resolved never again to swot for "Trials,"
except by himself or with *one* other fellow, and he
carried out his resolution for the few remaining
"Trials" that term.

In "Trial-rep" he was very lucky; but his *vivâ-
voce* Euclid cost him some trouble. But what were all
his labours when, at the beginning of next term, he
found he had secured his much desired "Remove"?

CHAPTER XI.

RATS.

"RATS!
They fought the dogs, and killed the cats,
And bit the babies in the cradles,
And ate the cheeses out of the vats,
And licked the soup from the cook's own ladles,
Split open the kegs of salted sprats,
Made nests inside men's Sunday hats,
And even spoiled the women's chats,
By drowning their speaking
With shrieking and squeaking,
In fifty different sharps and flats.

*　　*　　*　　*　　*　　*

Great rats, small rats, lean rats, brawny rats,
Brown rats, black rats, gray rats, tawny rats."

BROWNING'S "*Pied Piper of Hamelin.*"

IT was the middle of Easter term; "footer" just over, and running, about to begin regularly. Our hero stood at the house door in deep thought. The previous night he had had his patience sorely tried by a rat hunt in his room. Just as he was going to his press to get out a clean shirt for next day, a big piebald rat had jumped out of the lowest shelf, and run off under the bed. Just then

the gas went out suddenly (as it always did about
10.15), so Russell, fearing to tread with bare feet on
the floor, and having no matches, had sat, half un-
dressed on his bed, in terror of an assault. At last,
in walked his tutor, candle in hand. The two,
aided by Lyon, had had an unsuccessful hunt, and the
master, half suspecting that the rat was imaginary,
and an excuse for Russell's not being in bed, went
off, leaving our hero still in a deadly funk. He had
passed a wretched night; for the animal kept scrambling about, now here, now there, and whenever our
hero dropped asleep it was to dream of rats. At
last he took courage to climb over the table to the
door, which he set open, in the hope that his visitor
would take the hint. Not a bit of it; and after an
hour or so, Lyon, whose bed was nearest the door,
declared he wouldn't stand the draught any longer.

The rat had not been found yet. "What if it
should die, and make a stink behind my hat-box!"
thought Russell. But greater troubles were in store
for him.

The animal, it seemed, had escaped from No. 18,
a room belonging to two small fellows who kept
quite a menagerie. They had a guinea-pig, three
white rats, two piebald rats (of which Russell's dis-
turber was one), a cage full of white mice, and a
family of dormice, which lived in Henderson's "Ex-
bag." None but the owners, Henderson and Scrapfield could enter the room, without being nearly
knocked down; the monkey-house at the Zoo was
nothing to it. It was stated that Scrapfield always
had three or more mice in his jacket pocket, and it
was quite certain that one had walked out one
evening on to the hall-table at prayers. Henderson

once took a white rat into school, but the Master
"twigging" it, watched his opportunity, "nailed"
it in the paper-basket, and sent its owner home with
his rat, *plus* two hundred lines. The rat and mouse
nuisance was getting too much of a good thing in
the house. "Find"-cupboards were infested and
pillaged, rooms scented, fellows tormented, boots
nibbled, collars devoured. But the whole affair
came to a climax when Russell, the night after his
rat-hunt, having satisfied himself that the room was
clear, got into bed, and found something gnawing at
his toes. Whether by accident or design, two white
rats had found their way between the sheets.

Next day, roused by complaints on all sides, a
council of Sixth-form fellows was held, to determine
what steps should be taken to abate the nuisance.
The Head of the House presided, and in his room
the council met. Before long they resolved themselves into a committee of inquiry, and in the
evening marched in state into No. 18, holding their
noses. They found the room in a fearful state of
untidiness. The table was thrust into a corner; a
broken chair lay in the fender; and Henderson sat
in the middle of the floor, trying to force something
that looked like mud into the guinea-pig's mouth,
with a spoon. He looked rather startled on the
entrance of the authorities, but continued his efforts
with the struggling animal. "What are you doing
to that poor brute?" asked the Head of the House,
speaking from behind a handkerchief saturated with
eau-de-cologne. "Oh, I didn't think Samuel had
been quite well lately," replied Henderson, "so I'm
giving him some medicine." "What is your beast-
liness made of?" interposed another of the Sixth

form. "Oh, it is bread and mustard and sugar
and water, with some camphor." "No wonder the
beast won't eat it, then!" replied the questioner;
"Where is Scrapfield?" "He is gone to the tap
for hot water, because it is Arthur's bath-night."
"Who may Arthur be?" asked the Head of the
House. "Why, Arthur is the biggest piebald rat."
"Oh, the brute I caught in my coal-scuttle!" remarked some one. "How many beasts have you
altogether?" continued the Head, sniffing at his
handkerchief. "Well, let's see; five rats and the
guinea-pig, thirteen white mice, and seven dormice.
And then Scrapfield has bought a rabbit, which is
to live under his bed." "Where do the rest of the
brutes live?" "Oh, the mice have a cage, and the
dormice are in an ' Ex - bag,' and the rats are in
the wash-hand-stand cupboards, and the guinea-
pig—the guinea-pig——." "Well, speak out;
where does the guinea-pig live?" "Why, he *used*
to live in my clothes-press, before he was ill."
"Yes, and where does he live now?" "Well,"
(this reluctantly), "he sleeps in my bed now!" A
roar of laughter greeted this confession. "Where
did you get all the beasts?" pursued the Head.
"Oh, chiefly through the *Exchange and Mart ;* we
answer the advertisements." "Are *all* the brutes
in the room just now?" asked one of the Sixth
form, with a sort of shudder. "All except one of
the white rats, and we don't know where he has got
to." "I do, though!" exclaimed a new-comer,
catching the words; "he is down in your 'Find '-
cupboard, eating ham," turning to the Head of the
the House. "By jove! is he though?" and with
that the irate Head turned, followed by the others,

Henderson bringing up the rear, praying that mercy
might be shown to the culprit.   Sure enough, there
was the white rat in the cupboard.   Nobody would
touch it but Henderson, who embraced it tenderly,
and retired with it in his arms.   Then, after burning
a pastille in the " Find "-cupboard, the committee
sat, and called in witnesses, one by one.   First came
Russell, who recounted both his experiences.   Then
came Crawdon, who deposed that on Saturday night
he had come into his room, and (in the fullest sense
of the words) had " smelt a rat."   That on his going
for the fire-irons to attack the animal, if he could
discover it, he had found one of his slippers entirely
spoilt by being torn and gnawed.   The next witness
proved that on three separate occasions his sleep
had been disturbed by mice, while a fourth alleged
that the contents of his " Find "-cupboard, viz., a
chicken, a tongue, two pots of jam, some tinned
meat, and a packet of sugar, had been rendered
" unfit for human food," by the depredations of rats.
Other witnesses told of the destruction of books,
clothes, etc.   After all the witnesses had retired, the
council laid their heads together, finally deciding
that the obnoxious animals must be removed.   *How*,
was the question.   To take them by force from the
owners would be no easy matter ; besides, no one
liked touching them.   It was a case requiring deep
consideration.   That night, the Head of the House,
having put some more eau-de-cologne on his handkerchief, paid another visit to the room, and told
Henderson and Scrapfield that if the menagerie was
not disposed of in twenty-four hours, the Sixth form
would forfeit the whole stock of animals.
     But two days having passed, and the offenders

having disregarded the warning, another council was held, which resulted in a plan of selling the animals to a respectable old pedlar, who said that he could dispose of them easily in the villages through which he passed. He was to come one day during first school, while Henderson and Scrapfield were " up ; " one of the Sixth form was to stay out on that day to receive the man, and make the bargain. And so it was that the owners of the animals one day returned from first school to find their room untenanted by a single guinea-pig, rat, or mouse. That night the Head of the House came round, and forbidding them to get any more beasts, on any pretence whatever, paid down half the sum realised by the sale, saying that the other half would be given to the cricket fund, after compensation for devoured food, etc., had been made to those who had suffered by the rats and mice.

Long afterwards Henderson and Scrapfield went about, mourning for their lost pets, but the house has not since been troubled with vermin. Russell, for weeks afterwards, made his bed afresh every night, to see if anything was to be found between the sheets. And, till the day he left, there stuck to him (the chief sufferer from the great nuisance) the nickname of " Rats."

CHAPTER XII.

DECORATIONS.

"Nay sir; but verily, as a garden without plants, as a hearth without a fire, as a speech without meaning, so is an apartment destitute of embellishment.

"I like it not; for, be it never so spacious, it lacketh comfort, and it is comfort that maketh the home."

SAYINGS OF SIR TITUS TRUTHSOME.

LYON and Russell were determined to make their room respectable, and not only respectable, but really handsome. It was the beginning of the summer term (following the term in which the events recorded in the last chapter took place); and, as Russell said, "It's worth while making your room jolly for summer term; partly because it is a long term, partly because there are no fires to make a mess; and then there is 'Speecher' too; one always likes the place to look decent on 'Speecher,' you know."

Accordingly, the first few days were in great part spent in getting the room respectable. It is wonderful how little things mount up. One buys a few dozen brass nails and tin tacks, but soon finds that more are wanted; the deficiency has to be supplied : about a score of fresh packets of these nails and tacks alone have to be bought before all is done. Then there is picture-cord and picture-nails, and baize and fringe, and perhaps a new mantel-board and a few new brackets to fill up odd spaces. So that, by the time Russell and Lyon had finished their decorations, they found that the money had flown wonderfully. Still, they had reason to be satisfied with the result. To begin with, at the end of last term they had made a petition to the Matron, that had resulted in their having an almost new carpet, and a respectable cloth for the middle table. Then Lyon had a small side-table, a legacy from some fellow who had left, and he had brought a table-cloth from home for it.

They were well off for pictures, Russell having half a dozen hunting scraps, neatly framed, a few photographs of scenery, several heads of dogs and horses, and three of those large prints of Landseer's best known paintings, which cover a great space, but are regular " art-murders."

Lyon had brought several very good oleographs from home, as well as some water-colour drawings done by his people. He also had four sporting pieces, and one or two good prints. Lyon did the picture hanging (with Russell's assistance when needed), while Russell undertook what he called the " tapestry and drapery department." He was determined not to confine himself to the unvarying monotony of red or green baize and fringe, so he went about the town to find something more out of the common. The shopkeepers, he thought, were-

very stupid. He asked to see baize of other colours
than red or green. No, they had none. Well, he
was not particular about its being baize; had they
any cloth or other material? No, none. He explained it was for covering mantelpieces or bed-door
panels. No, they had nothing that would do. At
last he turned to leave the shop in despair. Just
then, his eye lighted on something which looked
like dark-blue baize. "Hullo! what's this?" he
exclaimed. "That, sir, is blue flannel," replied the
shopman, rubbing his hands together. "Well, why
won't that do?" All the shopman could answer
was, that it wasn't usual to cover mantel-boards with
flannel, and that most gentlemen used baize.
"Didn't I tell you that I wanted something unusual
and different from what most gentlemen use?" cried
Russell. So he purchased some blue flannel, and
the shopman, with the air of one who is amusing a
child or humouring an idiot, then produced some
material of a rich violet hue, though he stated that
he didn't think gentlemen had ever asked for it
before. Russell was much taken with it, and bought
some. He returned in triumph to the house. When
all was finished it looked very well. The inside
window sill, which was very unsightly, being cut and
stained with ink, was covered with blue flannel with
red fringe (he could not get blue); and the bed-door
panels were covered with violet stuff fastened on with
grand star-pattern brass nails. The mantel-board
was covered, later on in the term, with a worked
affair from home, but, for the first few weeks, it was
done in violet with red fringe.

Then they got several brackets, and on them and
the mantelpiece placed various ornaments, of which

the most striking was a china figure of a gentleman
in blue, sitting on the edge of a large gilded shell of
fabulous shape. Next they purchased a fire-ornament—one of the "cascade" pattern; but the very
night it was put up, Russell thoughtlessly, from sheer
habit, flung the match he had struck to light the gas
with into the fender, and in a moment the fire-ornament was in a blaze, nearly setting the chimney on
fire, and singeing the fringe of the mantelpiece.
However, after three or four ornaments had perished
in this manner, they were cured of the trick, and
managed to keep one unhurt till the end of the term.
Russell wrote home for muslin curtains, which were
not, however, put up till a little before " speecher,"
lest they should get dirty before that eventful day.
After all the decorations were completed, Russell and
Lyon bound themselves to abide by the following
regulations :—

(1.) That they should take it in turns to sweep the
floor (maid's sweeping goes for nothing), shake the
table-cloths, and eradicate grease spots from the
mantelpiece once a week.

(2.) That neither of them should leave his books,
clothes, etc., about the room.

(3.) That they should, as much as possible, prevent other fellows from smashing their ornaments,
or making a mess about the room.

But, faithfully as they kept to these agreements,
accidents did occur. Fellows *would* come and play
" footer " in the room during their absence, or
borrow books from the shelves and pull down all the
rest to get at the particular ones they wanted. So

that a broken picture-glass or ornament, or an upset
of ink on the table-cloth, were not rare occurrences.
Then the maid would always arrange their furniture
to her own taste, which was not identical with theirs.
Nevertheless, on "Speecher" the room presented a
truly gorgeous appearance. Besides their own
ornaments they had borrowed several from fellows
whose people were not coming down. Then the
muslin curtains and worked mantel-cover were in
their glory. Cleanliness and neatness reigned
supreme. Pots of ferns stood in the fender in front
of the fire-ornament. As "Speecher" was a blazing
hot day, it was quite a treat to come into the room.
By a judicious arrangement of opening the windows
in the morning (when the sun was on the other side
of the house), and with the help of blocks of ice in
the washhand-basins, the temperature was delightful.
As to flowers, the table appeared to be one mass of
them ; they had spent quite a fortune at Naylor's.

They were most artistically arranged in vases,
tooth-glasses, and soap-dishes, and even in the cup
belonging to a travelling flask, which had been
pressed into the service. On each bouquet hovered
gorgeous butterflies (tropical ones, secured by a
little gum in natural positions on the flowers),
while a refreshing little fountain occupied one of
the presses. This was Lyon's idea ; it was supplied
from a jug on the top of the bookshelf above, by an
indiarubber tube.

Their people were quite enchanted, and seemed to
think that their hopeful sons did all their work
amid this blaze of flowers and butterflies and
fountains—in fact, in a sort of fairyland. If they
had looked into the next room (which belonged to

fellows whose people were not expected), a broken table, a three-legged chair lying on the ground, a smashed jug, a pool of ink, and an accumulation of jam-pots, would have met their eyes, and their ideas of life at Harrow would have been rudely dispelled.

CHAPTER XIII.

ANOTHER SUMMER TERM.

"When Bill plays at cricket,
  No ball on the green
Is shot from the wicket
  So sharp and so clean;
He stands at his station
  As strong as a king,
When he lifts up a nation
  On Victory's wing."

FROM "MUSA BURSCHICOSA."

HAT Summer Term was peculiarly delightful to our hero. His last summer, it will be remembered, was spoilt by his sudden removal to the "Sanny." But this year no such calamity marred his pleasure. At cricket he greatly distinguished himself, and, before long, got into "Sixth-form Game." He had no chance of his "flannels" *that* year, but many looked on him as a future player at Lords. He was one of the house bowlers, bowling being his strong point.

The first house match was played on a whole holiday, and began after "eleven bill." Great was

the excitement. Belfield was still the captain of
the Kingsfordites, and a very good captain he made.
In the first innings he made 68, not out; their total
being 149. Then the other side went in, and came
out for 150. In his second innings, Belfield was
unlucky, and got run out for seven. Russell was
the man who was expected to make up for this misfortune. The first ball he made a fine hit to leg,
followed by another and another. The score was
running up. The enemy put on other bowlers, but
to no purpose. By the time five wickets were down
he had made 52. Fellows came from all parts of
the field to look on. The shouting was tremendous.
Mr. Kingsford, himself a good player in younger
days, paces excitedly up and down, ever and anon
giving vent to his feelings by a shout of " Well hit,
sir ! " Russell seems invincible. At last, playing
perhaps a little carelessly, he sends the ball flying
right up in the air. " Whew ! " exclaims Mr. Kingsford, stopping in his walk, as he follows the ball
with his eyes, "out for certain ! " One of the
"fields" runs forward and catches it——No! he
juggles with it for a moment and then drops it.
Russell is still safe. A roar of derision and dis-
appointment bursts from friend and foe respectively,
at this incident. Then another steady spell of luck
for our hero, and he carries his bat for 72, no mean
contribution to the total score of 197.

It was too late to play out the match, but on the
Monday evening after, play was resumed. Russell's
bowling proved deadly. Five wickets fell to him,
including the adversary's best man, cut off in his
prime. Their total score was 98, leaving Kingsford's easily victors. Nor was Russell less dis-

7

tinguished in the next house match, which, however,
they just lost.

Time passed wonderfully quickly, and soon came
the little succession of events that proclaims the
approach of " Speecher. "   First " Governors'
Speecher," that time-honoured ceremony.   What
Harrovian recalls it not ?   The whole school assembled in " Speecher ; " a sort of irregular bill called ;
the announcement from the head master that " it is
our custom to receive the governors standing, and
in perfect silence." Then the Head of the School,
arrayed in evening dress, goes to summon the
governors from the room where they are kept, and,
after they have entered and are seated, he begins his
Latin speech.   It is a beautiful sight to see the faces
of those among the governors and masters who care
to follow the discourse in the book,—how their
countenances light up at a joke or a happy allusion !
Then to watch the Sixth form, who, for the most
part, listen with a dignified grace, as if they took it
all in as easily as English.   Then, when the
" Contio " is over, come the long-suppressed cheers,
and the hand-shaking among the governors and
masters.   In a few days, after the rehearsals of the
actual " Speeches " before the townspeople and the
school, comes the great day itself.   Russell was up
early that day seeing to his room, the decorations of
which have been described in the last chapter.   His
people came down pretty early, and were enchanted
with the room.   Then they were conducted by our
hero to the various " lions " of the place.   On the
green, in front of the " Vaughan," played the Rifle
Corps band, in uniform, with colours flying.   After
visiting the chapel, schools, terrace, " Vaughan,"

etc., it was time to go into "Speecher." When he
had seen his people safely into seats, our hero came
out and strolled about with a few others, sat in the
chapel to hear the organ, and in various ways killed
time. He met several old Harrovians, to some of
whom he merely nodded; while with others he
walked about, according to his acquaintance with
them. There is Bowbury, who used to be in Kingsford's, he is at Cambridge now; and Brydges (by
Jove! what a moustache he has grown!); and Pilton
who looks like a man of thirty, though he only left
last term; and there (the fellow with the white top
hat and eye-glass) is "fop" Frankland; and there,
yes, *there!* is "Cousin Charlie," in great force, with
an alarming bouquet in his button-hole. How
happy they all look! Nobody can say that old
Harrovians lose their love for the old place. At last
it is time to go and cheer the visitors up in the
school-yard. (This was before *new* "Speecher" was
completed.) Russell, with several others, strolls up
and joins the throng of loungers sitting and standing
under the temporary awnings against the big wall.
At last the door of "Speecher" opens, and the company begins to pour out. The Head of the School
takes up his position on the steps, supported by one
or two masters, who nudge him when a "swell"
appears. Then the fun begins. "Three cheers for
Lord ——! Hip, hip, hip, hurrah!" cries the Head,
and ere the shouting has died away, "Three cheers
for the Bishop of ——." How pleased the good
Bishop looks as he smiles round on the sea of young
faces, and bows his thanks for the honour done him.
Then more "swells" and more cheers; now for a

brave officer, now for a solemn judge, now for a
learned College Don, now for a noble lord.   See that
dear stout old gentleman with the benign spectacled
face; how delighted he looks.   How he bows, and
smiles, and lifts his hat, little thinking that the
cheers are not for *him*, but for the thin, nervous-
looking celebrity, who has hurriedly passed down the
steps scarce noticed, but whose name it is that has
been the key-note of the shouting.   More lords and
ladies, more bishops and judges, more officers and
travellers!   The throng seems endless.   The Head
of the School is quite hoarse, and so is everybody.
At last Russell sees his people, joins them, and they
go back to the house.   A short time is spent in the
gorgeous room described in Chapter XII. and then
comes the "spread" in hall.   The room looks quite
gay, with garlands, etc., and over the fireplace is a
grand scroll with "*Stet fortuna domus*," the school
motto, emblazoned on it.   Mr. Kingsford is busy
"doing the host," while the clatter of knives and
forks and the hum of conversation is incessant.
Why linger to detail the proceedings ?

After the "spread" and a little more lionising,
the Russells go off in their carriage (for they have
driven down from London).   When he has seen
them off, our hero meets more old schoolfellows, and
contrives to pass the time till the sun gets low and
the visitors scarce, when he joins the throng of
bathers at "Ducker," and enjoys a dip after the
heat and glare and excitement of the day.

Summer term is a succession of excitements great
and small, and as soon as "Speecher" is over,
every one begins to think of Lords and Wimbledon.

Of these the first deserves a separate chapter; to
the last Russell, although a member of the Rifle
Corps, was not going, having devoted his time to
cricket, to the exclusion of the drills, etc., necessary
before being put on the Wimbledon list. But
although he was not going, he felt very patriotic on
the morning of the day when he saw the 'busses,
loaded with Rifle Corps fellows in uniform, start
with colours flying and band playing; and when
they returned that night with the glorious news
that the Ashburton shield was still to adorn the
walls of the "Vaughan," he felt as proud as if he
had been on the spot.

Quite at the end of the term, after Lords, came a
spell of wet weather, such as even the oldest inha-
bitants never recollected to have occurred at that
time of year. The cricket pitches were a swamp,
the open racket and fives courts were inundated;
nothing could be done, except, indeed, in the gymnasium. Some one suggested "footer," and though
the idea was novel, several "voluntary" games
were well attended, and our hero was not slow to
join them. Nor did a rush and a plunge in
"Ducker," clothes and all, at the conclusion of the
game, lessen its attractions; and this proceeding,
supplemented, as it always was, by a run up the
hill and a hot bath, failed to produce the "death of
cold" which the worthy matron predicted. One
day Russell, finding swimming in foot-ball boots
rather hard work, took them off before he went into
the water; but his stockings were so wet after the
immersion, that putting on the boots when he came
out was out of the question; so he had to run home

without, whereby his stockings and feet were not a little cut about.

The wet weather lasted till the end of the term, but fortunately did not extend over the holidays, which our hero spent travelling on the Continent.

CHAPTER XIV.

LORDS.

 CROWD of fellows—the whole school, in fact—upon the green, under the swinging sign of the "King's Head," one bright summer morning. The stranger asking the meaning of this concourse will be told that every one has turned out to see the Eleven start for Lords, whither they drive in the coach that stands before the inn-door. At length they appear, in twos and threes, and mount to their seats, ready to start. Strong, gentlemanly young fellows all of them, in their sombre, plain clothes; you will hardly recognise them a few hours later, in their white flannels and dark-blue sashes, playing at Lords. Yet these humble-looking individuals are

the heroes of the two days, not only among their schoolfellows, but before fashionable London (perhaps Royalty), before the cricketing world; their names will appear in every newspaper, thousands of eyes will be upon them, their every action will be the signal for a shout. (Courteous reader, if you are not an Harrovian, forgive the feeling which prompts this, perhaps, overdrawn description.) Off they go, and as the coach disappears down the London road, in a cloud of dust, a loud cheer rises from the crowd, heartily answered from the departing coach. Then every one goes back to breakfast; then comes an early second school, and then a rush for the station. Over this scene of confusion let us pass, and imagine ourselves at the gate of Lords.

A hansom drives up, and three youths alight. After the usual abuse from the cabman, they show their dark-blue tickets, and go on to the ground. Who is this in such elegant attire? No other than our hero; and his two companions are Lyon and Vernon, both equally spruce. Mark the white waist-coats and new trousers that have lately been the subject of grave discussion over Winkley's or Con-ways's counter; mark, too, the kid gloves and fault-less top-hats; and last, but not least, the fashionable sticks, with their dark-blue tassels, selected, no doubt, after deep deliberation, from the extensive stock laid in by the enterprising "Gus."

"Come on; let's try and get a seat in front," exclaims Russell; and forthwith they make a rush for the ropes, where, after a short time, they get good places, and settle themselves to watch the play. Harrow is in, and some good hitting is taking place. "I wonder who the Eton wicket-keep is?"

says Vernon. "Oh, that's—let me see" (referring
to his card)—"that's Godfrey," answers Russell.
"No, it isn't," says Lyon ; " Godfrey is that dark
fellow at cover-point, because my brother knows his
cousin, and——well *hit*, sir; well hit ! By Jove !
did you see. that ? " With such rambling conversation the time passed on till lunch-time arrived,
when Russell and Vernon went off in search of food,
and Lyon, more fortunate, got his in a carriage
belonging to some friends on the ground. After the
two others had satisfied their hunger and thirst,
they found that play had been continued. The
ground was now too crowded to give any chance of
their getting a front seat, and they commenced a
fruitless walk round, in search of any place where
they could get a glimpse of the wicket. At last the
innings is completed, and the crowd spreads out
over the greensward. Everybody meets everybody
else, then everybody strolls up to see the pitch being
rolled, and soon the bell rings, and in a marvellously
short time the ground is once more clear. Then
again the bursts of applause and the click of the
bat continue, till the sloping rays of the sun warn
the spectators that the day's play is at an end.

Next day saw our hero driving with his people
(who had places in the Grand Stand) to the scene
of action. "Card o' the match, sir ? " asks a card-
seller of Russell. "Yes ! " He looks at it anxiously,
almost forgetting to pay for the card in his excitement. Eton are all out, and the dark blue have just
gone in. Why detail our hero's doings that day ? It
was just yesterday over again, except a shower of
rain, by way of variation, and the consequent rush for
shelter. But it soon cleared up again, and Russell

was once more threading his way among the car-
riages in search of some friends, when a hand was
laid upon his shoulder, and, looking round, he saw
" Cousin Charlie " standing by his side, resplendent
in dark blue tie, and evidently much elated. " How
d'ye do, young man ! " he began ; " saw you in the
crowd yesterday, but couldn't catch your eye. All
flourishing, eh ? grand match, isn't it ? " With such
like exclamations, spoken in his loudest tones,
" Charlie " went on, till an unfortunate engagement
took him away leaving our hero to continue his
peregrinations. Lots of old schoolfellows he met ;
old Harrovians " most do congregate " at the Eton
v. Harrow at Lords.

Late in the afternoon the match is finished, leaving Harrow victors over a well-matched foe after a
closely-contested game. Loud are the cheers, hearty
the congratulations when all is over, and right proud
is the dark blue of its hard-won triumph.

I am fully aware that my description of a match
at Lords is feeble in the extreme ; nevertheless, a
book about Harrow, without mention of Harrow's
greatest annual event, would be incomplete, and I
must fall on the reader's forbearance, if my grovelling
pen has in any way rendered tedious a subject
which soars above my humble powers.

CHAPTER XV.

RUSSELL'S "FIND."

" *Petruchio :* What is this? mutton?
1*st Servant :* Ay.
Pet. : Who brought it?
1*st Serv. :* I.
Pet.: 'Tis burnt; and so is all the meat!"
SHAKESPEARE'S *" Taming of the Shrew."*

ET me explain to the uninitiated the meaning of the word at the head of this chapter. A " Find " in Harrow *parlance* signifies a party of two or more who club together to take their breakfast and tea in the room of one of their number, instead of going for those meals, as the lower boys do, into Hall. In some houses, the Sixth form only are allowed to be on a " Find," but in others (of which Kingsford's was one), the Fifth form are also eligible. And so it came about that when our hero reached the second Fifth form, he was put on a " find " consisting exclusively of Fifth-form fellows, who had to do their own fagging ; and in the following term, having reached the first Fifth he was transferred to another which had a Sixth-form fellow on it, so that he, and the two

other Fifth-form boys on the "find," though unable
actually to practise fagging, had all the benefit of
using Elsworthy's fags. At least so they maintained,
though the fags didn't see it in the same light. One
of the fags, Smith minor, was especially rebellious.
"I am not your fag, but Elsworthy's," he would
remark when Russell told him to go up town for
hot meat. "No, you're not ; you're the fag on No. 15
find," our hero would reply.   But, in spite of these
little disagreements, the members of the "find" got on
very well with their fags, who were four in number,
coming into office in order, for a week each.

Elsworthy was a merry sort of fellow, who didn't
do much work, and had taken his time to reach the
sixth form ; the other members were Lyon, Vernon,
and Russell. At the beginning of the term they framed
a set of rules, which were hung up inside the "Find"
cupboard, and of which the following is a copy.

RULES OF No. 15 FIND.

I. That every member of the "find" shall pay to
the Treasurer, at the commencement of the term,
a subscription of £1, to be expended in hot meat,
jam, potted meat, rolls, etc., for the use of the
"find."
II. That when this sum is all spent, there shall
be a further *voluntary* subscription not exceeding 10s.
per head, and the "find" shall take care to live more
frugally for the rest of the term.
III. That any member wishing to introduce a
visitor to a meal, shall give due notice beforehand.
IV. That any member misbehaving at table, or
talking "shop" (except in "Trial" week) during

meals shall be fined twopence, or rolls to that amount.

V. That any member bringing anything except a newspaper to read at table, shall be fined one penny.

VI. That the fags be kept in due order by the Sixth-form member, and that they be denied all "perquisites" except lump sugar in moderation.

VII. That any member making a mess on the table-cloth, or buttering the furniture, shall be fined threepence.

VIII. That all fines (if not paid in rolls) shall be handed over to the Treasurer.

IX. That if any member smashes any furniture or crockery, he shall pay for it when it appears in the "breakage list."

X. That members be expected occasionally (on whole holidays, *etc.*) to subscribe to a grand break-fast, to which visitors shall be invited.

XI. That any member who persistently sings, shouts, whistles, talks bosh, or otherwise renders himself offensive, shall be kicked down the passage, and excluded from the next meal on the "find."

XII. That the Treasurer every Saturday night take care to provide sufficient cold meat, *etc.*, for Sunday.

We the Undersigned do agree to abide by these rules :—

G. F. ELSWORTHY (Sixth Form).

W. R. LYON (Treasurer).

H. RUSSELL.

D. A. VERNON.

These rules were most faithfully adhered to ; the

seventh rule was always bringing our hero into trouble, but he paid up, each time he violated it, with a very good grace. Those meals on the "find," how luxurious they were! Not as regards the food so much as the manner of taking it—the genial conversation—the discussion over the newspaper—the total exclusion of all the cares of work—the business-like concentration of all the energies on being comfortable. However cold the evening was, a roaring fire cheered the " find "-room, before which lay (according to the state of the funds) steaming dishes of savoury fish, flesh, and fowl, or the more frugal plate of hot-buttered toast and crumpets. However much trouble had fallen on any of the members during school—after one good grumble, all care was cast aside during the cheerful meal. The meat might be (but it was not often) tough, or the eggs antique; but these trifles did not disturb the minds of the four philosophers bent upon jollity. "Give it to the fag," was the invariable formula spoken over any food unfit for human consumption.

Never was there a pleasanter party: Elsworthy the witty, Lyon the dense and good-natured, Russell the boisterous, and Vernon the musical. Their little differences in politics were sufficiently keen to create discussion without animosity ; in this too, they were pretty well divided, two a side, Elsworthy and Russell being Conservatives, and the other two Liberals. It was wonderful what a patriotic feeling they had for the old " find " room, with its red curtains and spacious " find "-cupboard ; it was Vernon's room, shared with a fellow in the Remove, who took breakfast and tea in hall, and was promptly ejected if he showed his nose in the " find "-room during

meal time. It was rather hard lines on him being
kept out of his room, especially in the evening,
for they rarely sat over their tea for less than two
hours, talking and laughing. However, to make up
for it, he was often invited to take tea on Sunday, on
the " find."

" Well," said Vernon, coming into the "find"-
room for tea one miserable evening, putting his
dripping umbrella in a corner, and proceeding to
warm himself before the fire. " Well, this is enough
to make a fellow vow that he'll never look at a 'con'
again!" " Why, what's the row?" asked Elsworthy,
who was making the tea. " Well, I did that ' con '
right through (it isn't *often* I do), and knew every
word of it, and now I've got to write it all out, Greek
and English, and do fifty lines besides, all because I
couldn't parse some beastly verb!" " Well," said
Russell, " I'm very sorry for you, but it's time for
tea now, not grumbling; so let's begin. There's
cutlets and sausages to-night!" So with a good
grace, Vernon cast his care away, and soon they
were hard at work on the hot meat. " I say," says
Elsworthy at last, " what do you say to giving a
fags' feast?" " A fags' feast?" exclaimed Russell
and Vernon in a breath. " Yes, a fags' feast; old
Baker gave the fags on his 'find' a spread last
term, and they worked all the better for it." " Oh,
it'll make them fat and lazy, and they'll get so
familiar and cocky too," said Lyon. " We must prevent that," replied Elsworthy; "no need of our
talking to them much,—just let them feed well, that's
all; and as to its making them lazy, I don't believe
it." " But are we to sit and watch them feed?"
asked Vernon. " Well, that depends; it would be

rather *infra dig* to sit down with them to tea." "Oh,
I don't know," said Russell; "we can keep dignified;
and besides I don't see the fun of our going without
tea just because we're too grand to sit down with
them." "Perhaps you are right," replied Elsworthy,
"but we must keep awfully dignified, or else they *will*
get cocky, and think they need never do any fagging."

After a long discussion it was agreed that a fags'
feast should be given, and Elsworthy, with his
customary formality, drew up the following notice
which he stuck up inside of the door of the "find"-
cupboard, or, as he called it, the "notice board."
As will be seen, admittance to the banquet was by no
means unconditional, indeed, everything was ordered
under most stringent regulations. The document
ran as follows :—

"Whereas it has been decided to give the fags of
No. 15 Find a fags' feast, the same will be given
on Wednesday fortnight at tea-time. The following
only are allowed to come,—Smith minor, Kinross,
Dale, and Burlington junior. They must receive
from Mr. Elsworthy certificates (duly signed by all
the members of the ' find ') of good conduct, activity,
civility, *etc.*, for the last three weeks. Without such a
certificate none will be admitted. Any complaint on
the part of the gentlemen of No. 15 will result in
the exclusion of the fag complained of. N.B.—The
fags must come to the feast, clean ; and any fag misbehaving at table will be kicked out."

Wednesday fortnight saw the "gentlemen of No.
15" standing round the fire in the "find-room,"
"waiting," as Elsworthy remarked, "to receive the
tenantry." Suddenly, the door was burst open, and

in flew Kinross, hotly pursued by Burlington junior.
"Hullo! I say," cried Russell, "just you go back,
and come and knock at the door properly, or you
shan't come to the spread at all." Accordingly,
with much laughter, but with some show of submission, the irrepressible pair departed, and soon
re-entered, accompanied by the other fags, in a most
decorous fashion. The table had been lengthened by
the addition of a small side table, rather higher than
was comfortable, but still imposing. At this, Elsworthy presided, making tea, while Russell took the
lower end, Lyon and Vernon (both with a fag at each
elbow), occupying the sides. By this arrangement
the fags were separated, having all of them a
patron on each side. To make them feel still
smaller, the fag-masters sat on elevated seats (*i.e.*,
chairs with big dictionaries to make them higher).
The conversation was certainly constrained, for the
members of the "find" were so dignified as to be ill at
ease, while the fags—well, a hungry fag, with a good
plateful of food before him, is no brilliant conversa-
tionist. The bill of fare was:

Tea.	Cocoa.
Fish Cutlets.	
Rolls and Jam.	
Roast Chicken.	
Potted Tongue.	Honey.
Sardines.	
Bread and Butter.	

I have adhered to the *order* as nearly as possible.
When the meal was over, and the fags were satisfied, the talk flowed a little more easily. The fags,
having fed, had time to look about them; and
Kinross, for the first time, observed the method by
which the members' seats were constructed. " I
say," he exclaimed, with a cheeky grin, addressing
himself to Smith minor, who sat opposite; " these
fellows have to have books stuck on their chairs, just
ike babes in the nursery ! " " Hold your row !" replied Elsworthy, reddening, with a dignified frown.
" Oh, I say, isn't he solemn ? " cried the irreverent
Burlington; "he looks as if he'd swallowed a
poker ! " " He's only ' stodged ' with rolls, he'll be
all right soon." This last remark, coming from
Dale, a great fat fellow who was nearly " lag " of the
school, caused a roar of laughter among the fags;
for Dale's speeches were few and far between, and
were not usually very brilliant. " If you fellows
can't behave, you'll be kicked out," said Vernon
severely, repressing a smile. " Oh, we don't mind,"
was the careless reply ; " we've had our tea now, and
we'll go as soon as you like." This was too true ;
they had got all they came for, viz., food ; and now
they were ready, if not impatient, to be off. All
Elsworthy's precautions had been in vain, and the
dignity of the " find " was suffering, nay, being held
to open ridicule. What was to be done ? Suddenly
a bright thought struck Russell. " Look here," he
said, scowling fiercely round the table, " this will be
the last feast we give if you can't behave." " Well,
you never meant to give another," remarked Dale,
quietly ; " at least not this term." This was quite
true, and rather floored our hero for a moment, but

he quickly replied, "Next term, though, we meant
to give another, but we shan't now, unless you hold
your insolent row." "Oh, as to next term," answered Burlington, unconcernedly, "Smith and I
shall be out of fagging, and Kinross and Dale have
promised to be fags on Fosser's 'find' next term,
so we don't mind what arrangements you choose to
make."

     *   *   *   *   *

"No," said Russell, thoughtfully to Vernon, as
he said good-night to him, a few hours later, "no;
I don't think we'll give another fags' feast."

CHAPTER XVI.

A "STOPPED EX."

"He is a wise man, who, even when Fortune is against him, seeks to make the best of adversity; who, when others would frown, ceaseth not to smile, and if he have naught better to laugh at, diverteth himself with the thought of how little his troubles afflict him."

SAYINGS OF SIR TITUS TRUTHSOME.

ES, Russell's "Ex" was *stopped;* and he was most indignant. But no arguments would alter Mr. Kingsford's determination. "If you choose to throw dirty water out of the window, when I happen to be passing underneath, you must expect to have your Exeat stopped," was all that our hero could get out of his tutor.

So finding appeal was useless, he went to his room, and wrote home as follows:—

"My dear Father,—

"I am very sorry that I shall not be able to come to you for the Exeat, as I have had a little misunderstanding with Mr. Kingsford; and as he seems to wish it, I have agreed to stay here for the Exeat, and I daresay that we shall soon be as good

friends as ever. I am really sorry that Mr. Kingsford should have made this mistake, since he is
usually very reasonable, as Masters go. The weather
is fine here. I hope you are all quite well. Give
my love to dear Mother, and the girls, and believe
me, Your affectionate son,

H. RUSSELL."

After posting this letter he felt quite relieved, and
indeed rather looked forward to the novelty of an
Exeat at Harrow, where he had never spent one
before.

There were eight fellows in the house who were
not going for the " Ex." Among them were Leigh,
Burlington junior, and Dale, names not unfamiliar
to us, and also O'Corke, a queer sort of chap, in the
" Shell," who delighted in mechanics, engineering,
etc. The only Sixth-form fellow left during the
" Ex," was Grimes, a small and unimportant individual, who had come into the school only a year
ago, and who, having got over every one's head so
quickly, was looked upon by most fellows as a " conceited young ass ; " it may therefore be imagined
that his influence was *not* great.

When the last cab had disappeared down the street,
on the Friday evening, Russell and Leigh turned
from the window out of which they had been looking,
and strolled into the Hall. There was no regular
" lock-up " call that night, but Mr. K. looked in to
see that every one was there. After an uncomfor-
table tea with Leigh and a Fifth-form fellow named
Jacobson, our hero sauntered round the house in
search of amusement. Most of the rooms were in
darkness, but at last he saw a light gleaming from

under a door, and immediately made for it. It was
O'Corke's room, a comfortless single room without a
fireplace, popularly known as "the Den."

Opening the door suddenly, Russell nearly knocked
down O'Corke, who was bending over a small boiler
at a table. "What have you got there?" demanded
our hero, seating himself on the window-seat, and
taking up a hammer that was lying near, with which
he commenced to beat a vigorous tattoo on a Latin
Dictionary also close at hand. "Boiler," replied the
engineer laconically, without turning round. "How
do you work it?" "I'll show you in a minute," he
replied, lighting a candle and turning out the gas,
after which he produced an india-rubber tube which
he fitted on to the gas burner and lit at the end,
placing the flame under the boiler.

Russell sat in silence for a few moments, awaiting
the result. He had not long to wait. A loud ex-
plosion shook the room; he had a vision of spouting
water and clouds of steam; he saw O'Corke spring
a yard into the air, and then all was darkness. After
sitting stupefied for a moment, Russell perceived an
awful smell of escaping gas, and groped towards the
burner to turn it off. This done, he bethought him
of O'Corke. "I say, where are you? Are you hurt?"
he inquired. No reply but a groan. "Can't you
speak, and tell a fellow what's the row?" persisted
Russell. "Only a bit scalded," replied a voice from
under the table.

An hour later O'Corke was in bed, his face en-
veloped in cotton wool, and half-a-dozen fellows
round him, offering mixed sympathy and ridicule.
"I say, old chap, how did it happen?" inquired
Leigh; "I wasn't here to see the fun, but I heard a

row like a young volcano going off. Really, though,
I hope you're not much damaged." "Oh, I don't
mind about myself," replied the invalid, piteously,
"it's only my nose and mouth that are hurt; but
my beautiful new boiler is smashed all to bits, and
I only got it yesterday from Birmingham. It was
such a beauty!" "Why didn't you clap on the
safety-valve?" inquired Russell. "Oh, you know
nothing about boilers," said O'Corke. "Glad I don't,
if they're all like this," answered our hero. "Well,
good night, old fellow; hope you'll be all right to-
morrow." So saying, he departed, accompanied by
Leigh to his own room, where they spent the rest
of the evening together over roasted chesnuts and
biscuits.

It seemed queer to Russell going to bed alone in
his room; every moment he expected Lyon would
walk in, and he half envied that individual when he
thought that he was at that moment probably en-
joying himself at the play.

Next morning Russell "cut" nine-bill and took a
"froust;" this he thought a good idea, as it cost
him some "lines," the writing of which whiled away
a considerable part of an idle whole holiday. He
went down to a rather feeble game at football in the
afternoon, and walked over to the "Sanny" after
four-bill.

After "lock-up" and tea, our hero, with Leigh
and Burlington junior, wandered about the house, at
a loss what to do. Suddenly a bright thought struck
Russell. "Let's have a concert!" The very thing!
No sooner said than done. All the fellows in the
house were got together, except Grimes (whose Sixth-
form dignity disapproved of the whole proceeding)

and the unfortunate O'Corke (whose injuries still
kept him in bed).

The orchestra consisted of two *combs*, two *drums*
(baths thumped with pokers), a pair of cymbals (two
shovels clashed together), and a *conductor*. This last
official was Leigh, with a racket as a " *bâton*," which
he used occasionally rather forcibly on his unruly
band. Every one, except the *combs*, sang, or rather
shouted lustily. After a preliminary practice in
Russell's room, they proceeded to march in proces-
sion about the passages, playing " Bonny Dundee,"
" The British Grenadiers," and other airs of a lively
character. To perform this portion of the programme
the drummers used coalscuttles instead of baths, on
account of their being more portable.

During a pause, partly for breath, partly to settle
what melody should next be given, a timid voice
was heard : " Oh, you fellows, would you mind not
making such a row, please! " A roar of laughter
greeted this remonstrance on the part of Grimes, who
had joined them unobserved ; and some one defiantly
striking up " For he's a jolly good fellow," and the
air being speedily caught up by the rest with renewed
vigour, the temporary head of the house disappeared,
after a few efforts to make himself heard.

For a few moments the cavalcade proceeded on
their way unmolested, but suddenly, at the end of a
dark passage, there appeared a strange figure.
Every one stopped their music, and gazed, spell-
bound, at the advancing apparition. Clad from head
to foot in white, its head (which seemed of enormous
size) hidden from view in a mass of snowy drapery,
and holding in one hand a flickering candle, the
figure came towards them noiselessly. All at once

the truth dawned upon Jacobson. "Why it's
O'Corke!" he cried, and sure enough, bare-footed,
in his night-shirt, a towel round his bandaged head,
there stood the occupant of "the Den." Hearing
the row, as well he might, he had crept from his bed,
and come out to see what was the matter. Before
they had time to explain, the piteous voice of Grimes
was again heard, this time conveying a message
from Mr. Kingsford, who, not being musical, objected
to the concert. Drowning the unfortunate Head's
expostulation by hoots, the band was just striking
up "See the conquering hero comes!" when the
"conquering hero" appeared round the corner in the
shape of Mr. Kingsford, who dispersed the musicians
with a warning, that if he heard any more of the
concert he would issue invitations for "extra school"
to all the performers.

So ended the first and last concert of the season,
and the bandsmen, a little tired and hoarse, went off
in various directions to refresh themselves with
lemonade or cocoa in their rooms.

Russell was surprised on Sunday morning by
being asked to sing in the chapel choir. All the
choir, except two, were gone away for the Exeat,
but the substitutes acquitted themselves very credit-
ably.

In the afternoon, after a short scripture lesson, he
started off with Leigh for a walk along the Kenton
road. Finding two donkeys roaming at large by the
roadside, what was more natural than to capture
and mount them? The appearance of two fellows
in swallow-tail coats and top hats riding on asses
is somewhat strange, and so thought a crabbed old
countryman who was coming along the road. Think-

ing that there was something wrong, he took upon himself to interfere. "Hi, there, yer young rascals," he shouted, "come out o' that, will yer? Get off them there jackasses, or I'll teach yer better." "Just you try it on, old buck!" retorted Leigh, giving his steed a touch up with his knotted handkerchief, which had no effect, for the animal only shook his ears and continued browsing. "Gee up, Neddy!" cried Leigh, redoubling his efforts. But before the animal could be made to stir, the old rustic was at his side. "Now then master, just yer get off that there donkey!" he exclaimed wrathfully. Just at this moment a clattering of hoofs was heard, and, looking round, Leigh saw the other donkey galloping down the road towards Harrow, Russell holding on like grim death. His own steed, startled by the noise, began to kick ferociously, upsetting the aged bucolic into the ditch, and then proceeded to rid himself of his rider. Glad to escape from the countryman, whom he left swearing in the ditch, and anxious to see Russell's fate, Leigh ran as hard as he could down the road, just in time to catch sight of Russell, still bestriding the donkey (which, however, had come to a standstill), confronted by three of the masters, who were out for a walk. They were too much amused to give any punishment, and after a few facetious remarks about two-legged and four-legged donkeys, went on their way, but not until Russell had dismounted.

The two riders never heard or saw anything more of the old rustic; but, as Leigh observed, "he was too lively when he was in the ditch to have been badly hurt."

So ended the events of the Exeat; and next day,

when the two stood cool and comfortable before the house door, watching with pity the wretched Ex-goers returning, late, dusty, and heated, they were not so very sorry they had stopped at Harrow.

CHAPTER XVII.

SIXTH-FORM DIGNITY.

" The power of fagging belongs to both divisions of the Sixth Form, that is, to about the first eighty boys in he school. . . Fagging, in its main features, is at the worst tiresome, hardly menial, and never cruel."

ARTICLE ON "HARROW" IN
" The New Quarterly Magazine," (No. 23).

THE stranger passing any of the large houses at Harrow must be wonderfully puzzled by the stentorian roars which from time to time are heard from within their walls. These roars—"*calls*" as they are termed—proceed from the lungs of the members of the Sixth form, and are addressed to the fags, who soon learn the voices of their masters, and come accordingly. It is hard to represent in writing the sound emitted by a Sixth-form fellow in the act of calling; it is the word "*boy*" indefinitely prolonged, the call terminating with the caller's supply of breath.

One fine morning our hero stood in the passage outside his door, his hands in his pockets, his head thrown back, his mouth wide open, his face crimson. He was giving his first *call*. His admiring friends stood around, chaffing him on his newly-gained dignity, for he had just got into the Sixth form. The fag came, with a smile on his face, and Russell ordered him with an air of great importance "just to light the fire," as if he had been accustomed to give the command every day for years.

Before many days his voice ceased to sound strange to the fags, his " *call* " grew more emphatic, less quavering, and his manner more imposing.

The great difficulty was to preserve that solemn air in all his actions which he thought befitted a Sixth-form fellow. He set himself to the task of taming his high spirits with a will. Some one picked up a memorandum which was said to be in his handwriting, running as follows :—

N. B. Must not (1) Make a row in passages.

             (2) Loaf at the house door.

             (3) Be familiar with the fags.

Must   (1) Keep order in the house.

             (2) Snub the fags.

             (3) Look solemn always.

But he did not, luckily for his popularity, keep all these rules very scrupulously, and though he made the fags do their work, and kept fair order, he could never " do the solemn," for—

> " His dignity was like an inverted cone,
>   Wanting its proper base to stand upone."

He was as merry as ever, and when there was more
row than usual about the house, fellows always said,
" Oh ! it's only Russell trying to make some chaps
shut up making a row."

Russell would never consent to do what too many
Sixth-form fellows delight in, viz., do other people's
work.   He had quite enough to do with his own,
and if any fag came up to him with a " Please
Russell, will you just tell us this bit of 'con;' I
can't make it out," he usually left the room quicker
than he came, and just as wise.

As befitted his position, our hero now had a single
room, Lyon having left at the end of the previous
term.   Though the apartment was small, and not
handsomely fitted up, it was very comfortable, containing two "frousters," of which one had but one
arm, and the other none, but which looked nevertheless imposing.   He also had one of the large
" Liddell and Scott's Lexicons," which contributed
in no small degree to our hero's dignity.   Not that
he ever opened it, but it looked learned ; and it was
a nice little job for an unruly fag to cut fifty pages
of it with a large paper-knife which Russell kept for
the purpose.   On one occasion he gave a fag a his-
torical book to cut, and afterwards discovered that
the neatly folded maps with which the work was
embellished had also been carefully cut at the fold
right through the middle.

Let it not be supposed, however, that intellectual
pursuits entirely engrossed our hero's time.   It was
Easter term, and he set himself to running with a
will.   Every morning half-cooked steaks found their
way into his room and down his throat; every
afternoon saw him " doing " the "Pinner mile," or

going over the shorter course on the " Ducker road."
Although he started " scratch" in all the house
races, he came in first in the half-mile and second in
the mile; and he was induced by his friends to enter
for some school-races.

One dull afternoon after four-bill, accordingly, he
might have been seen at the starting-post of the
"mile," waiting for the sound of the pistol. It goes
off; they start. Five of them there are, but two
drop off before the half-mile is passed. Holdby, a
fellow in the School Cricket Eleven, and Faber, the
captain of the School Football, are our hero's opponents. Holdby leads by some yards, the two
others keep close together. Suddenly, just as they
turn the corner and come in sight of the crowd at
the winning-post, Holdby gives in,—he has not cal-
culated his strength, and is unable to finish. Faber
and our hero spurt simultaneously. " Russell !" cry
some of the bystanders ; " Faber, well run Faber !"
cry others, while not a few murmur " dead heat."
And dead heat it will be if they go on like this ; only
ten yards more, but Russell, putting all his strength
forward, breasts the tape, winner of "the School
Mile " by about two yards only. What cheers, what
congratulations, as our hero sits down to recover his
wind. " Well run, old fellow," exclaim half a dozen
familiar voices all round him. Mr. Kingsford comes
up and offers to drive him home, but he is all right
again, and refuses the offer with thanks ; and before
long is trotting back over the course, contentedly
sucking a lemon, accompanied by his friends.

Nor was our hero less lucky in other races ; and
many a handsome cup adorned his room by the end
of term.

One night our hero was sitting in his room after
the gas was out, going over some " con," when he
heard a tremendous row in the passage. His first
impulse (for he was not yet quite accustomed to
Sixth-form dignity) was to rush out and join in it ;
but a moment's reflection caused him to stalk
solemnly out at his door, candle in hand, and say in
a commanding tone ; " I say you, fellows—get to
your rooms, and shut up making this beastly row ! "
" Oh, please Russell, we're only having races ; it's
such fun." " Fun or no fun," said our hero, in-
wardly longing to join in the row, "just go to your
rooms, or I'll make you ! " Accordingly they dispersed, and Russell returned to his room.

But he had not been there many moments before
the row began again, louder than ever.

His dignity greatly insulted, he strode out with a
racket, and laid into the offenders liberally, effectually
dispersing them.

He had not, however, been a quarter of an hour in
his room, before a row of a different kind attracted
his attention. " Bump, bump, bump ; " something
being dragged down stairs, something pretty heavy
too. Suddenly a pause, followed by a succession of
quicker thumps ending in a crash. Whoever it was
had thought it less trouble to let his burden make
its own way to the bottom. Russell rushed out into
the darkness to see what was the matter, and in-
stantly measured his length on the floor, shooting
over some heavy obstacle. Getting up, *minus* some
of the skin with which Nature had furnished his
shins, he cried out angrily ; " What's all this row
about ? Who's there ? Get to your room, whoever
you are—or rather come with me, and have a taste of

my racket first." So saying, he retired with as much
dignity as his bruised shins would allow of, and proceeded to get the instrument of torture from its place
of honour on the wall. "Come on," he shouted,
"whoever you are,"—but no one came to receive the
punishment. Snatching up a candle, Russell went
out—this time more carefully—to find the offender.
He could see no one; on the floor lay the cause of
his calamity, a large hamper containing the dirty
boots of the fellows in the upper passage—or rather
some of them, for the fall down stairs had partly
emptied the hamper (which had no lid) of its contents; and there lay, in hideous confusion, big boots
and little boots, muddy boots, comparatively clean
boots, thick boots, thin boots, shoes, football boots,
etc., *ad libitum*. After gazing a moment on this wreck
of leather and mud, our hero again bethought him
of discovering the culprit. Suddenly he saw a dirty
face with a hideous leer, peeping round the corner of
the passage, its nostrils dilated, its eyes twinkling
with merriment, its lips compressed as if to contain
a struggling shout of laughter. At first Russell
could not imagine what the apparition was, but he
was not left long in doubt. After a loud guffaw, accompanied by the wildest gesticulations, out came
"Jeemes" the footman from his hiding-place round
the corner. "Ho, ho, ho," he gasped; "lor! didn't
I laaf jest, to see them blooming boots a' bowling
down the stairs—I let 'em go so neat—and then to
see Mister Russell a flyin' out for all the world like
a cracker; ho! ho! ho! down he came, O my good-
ness, such a smasher! an' I heard him there a'swearing softly to himself; and then back he goes to get
his blooming racket, thinkin' as he'd whop some of

9

the young gents; and bye and bye he comes out with his candle that savage, and first he sees the boots, and then he ketches a sight of me—oh! ho! ho! lor! Mister Russell, yer'll be the dith of me, yer will!"

Our hero could not help being amused at the man, and seeing several inquiring heads surmounting nightshirts appearing at the various doors down the passage, he turned on his heel, muttering something about "careless fellow," and once more entered his room, where he was soon nursing his wounded shins, preparatory to getting to bed.

This is but a sample of Russell's cares—hardly a day passed but his Sixth-form dignity was outraged and had to be avenged.

So true is the saying, "Uneasy lies the head that wears a crown."

CHAPTER XVIII.

CONCLUSION.

"There are always many matches going on during 'cricket quarter,' but the choice of the eleven is seldom finally disposed of until within a few days of the match at Lords. By this means the emulation between those who are trying for a place in the 'roll of heroes' is kept up, and the disposition of the honour is always regulated by the performance of those upon whom it is conferred."   R. PITCAIRN's "*Harrow School.*"

HY this unusual stir at " bill " ? Everybody seems to have come up to the schoolyard very early, and those of the Sixth form who have been called over stand aside instead of passing out at the gates. The bill-master looks pleased; he goes on calling: "Smith Maximus?" "Here, sir." "Russell?" Our hero's answer is drowned in a storm of clapping —hundreds of pairs of hands greet him as he runs forward and lifts his hat (see, it is a speckled one*)

* *The School Eleven only* are permitted to wear white flannel trousers, and their costume is completed by a dark-blue sash and tie, a straw hat speckled black and white, and a white flannel coat with brass buttons bearing the school device. The eleven cap is striped dark-blue and white.

in acknowledgment of the honour, and then disappears in the throng to receive renewed congratulations from his friends. Yes; Russell has "got his flannels" (that is, uninitiated reader, he has got into the School Cricket Eleven), and never did any one more thoroughly deserve the distinction. All the term his energy at cricket has been unflagging, and two nights before the "clapping up at bill" the captain "gave him his flannels." To tell the truth, his modesty somewhat dreaded the ceremony of being clapped; but now the ordeal is over, he looks radiant as he goes down the street with two or three companions, his new brass buttons shining in the sun.

It has been remarked that however obscure, retiring, or even unpopular a fellow may have been, as soon as he gets his flannels he becomes popular, and it is thought an honour to be among his friends. But Russell did not need honours to bring him friends, he was popular enough before; now, however, he feels of more importance, though his is a disposition which nothing can make conceited.

It was a happy summer term, his last term at Harrow, and the remembrance of it was a bright spot in his school memories after he had left. The matches in which he played, the runs he made, the old friends he met, the new friends he made among the strangers who came to play in different matches, all these things lent a charm enjoyable only by a member of the School Eleven.

Our hero's room at this closing period of his Harrow career was a sight. Its walls were covered with trophies of his skill in athletics of every sort. There hung his House Cricket Eleven cap, and his football belt and fez; there hung the dark-blue cap of the Philathletic Club, and the magenta and black coat and cap of the School Football Eleven; and, to crown all, there hung the dark-blue and white cap and the brass-buttoned coat. Besides these adornments might be seen the sword and cap which he wore as an officer in the Rifle Corps, while cups of all sizes and shapes betokened his prowess in running.

At Lords Russell made a very fair score, and Harrow was victorious, so his happiness suffered no check. Of course all the Eleven were clapped separately in the schoolyard a few days after the match.

The prospect of leaving was no pleasant one to our hero, and as the time approached he was quite melancholy. Not that his case was so bad as that of some other fellows in the Eleven, who would probably never have anything to speak of in the cricket way after they had left, for Russell was going to Oxford, where he might find a still wider field for his skill. But the thought of leaving the old place, of losing so many friends, some of whom he might never see again, and the prospect—yes, he could not deny that—the prospect of ceasing to be a schoolboy, all this filled him with a certain amount of sorrow.

But he finished off the term and his Harrow career in a very merry fashion, in which we may as well follow him.

It was the last Saturday of the term, a whole holiday, and a beautiful warm day. At a little after nine o'clock might have been seen, in the room over Winkley's, some twelve fellows, several of them in the Eleven, sitting down to a substantial repast. It was our hero's " leaving breakfast."

The bill of fare was varied, consisting of salmon, ducks, chickens, cutlets, curry, ham, beef, jam, tea, coffee, omelette, etc. ; but even these delicacies did not entirely put a stop to conversation, which was plentiful, and chiefly turned on that most appropriate theme, the approaching departure of the breakfast-giver.

"You must come down and see us, old fellow, next term," said one. "Yes, that I will," replied our hero, helping his neighbour to chicken for the fourth time. "I must try and get a game of 'footer.' It's a rummy feeling, that I'll never play in a house match again." "Oh, Russell, don't go doing the melancholy," exclaimed another speaker; "you're a lucky dog to have done with school; I only wish *I* were leaving instead of coming back to two more terms of Latin and Greek."

"Oh, you may say that *now*," answered Russell; "but when the time comes, you'll wish you weren't leaving, and would put up with the Latin and Greek, if you could have another year of cricket and football with your old friends. Besides, one gets to be fond of the dear old place, and I think a fellow who is glad to leave must be either a brute or an ass." "I feel just the same," remarked he of the four helps of chicken; "I am awfully sorry to leave, though I wouldn't have believed it a year ago." "I'm rather sorry," continued Russell, in a more cheerful tone, "that I am leaving without a taste of the birch; it seems as if one's education was not complete without it." Here followed a series of jests about the birch, and our hero having been cheated of his deserts. By this time the capacity of the eaters had at length failed, and after unlimited iced lemonade, a move was made to the schoolyard, where "bill" was just beginning.

Let us pass over a few hours, and imagine our-selves in the old Speech-room. The concert is about to begin. Fellows are scrambling to their places; the gallery is filling with old Harrovians; the performers are busy making their final prepara-tions. Seated with several other members of the Cricket Eleven up by the window that overlooks the road, we see our hero. The evening is sultry; the old casements, with their glowing coats of arms, are thrown open, and those who are sitting nearest lean out of them. Inside the room all is one hum of conversation, mingled with the impatient stamping of the audience. Suddenly a lull, followed by a burst of music, proclaims that the concert has com-menced. How they echo through the walls, those young voices!—some childish in their clearness, others manly in their deeper and more vigorous tones. Perhaps nowhere as at Harrow is school singing carried so far. Every one joins, every one feels each word that he is singing, and the old school songs ring forth year after year with a fresh-ness that awakes many a slumbering memory in the hearts of the listeners, whose schoolboy days are past.

Suddenly Russell (who has been making signs of recognition to Lyon, who is leaning over the red-baize parapet of the old Harrovians' gallery) finds that something is wanted of him. What is it? Nothing less than a solo. Yes, he, a popular mem-ber of the Eleven, *must* give them a verse of the Cricket Song. They will take no denial, and in a twinkling his friends have got him on his legs, and he is singing, with as much spirit as if he had never sung it before:

> " Crash the palaces, sad to see ;
> Crash and tumble the courtiers three !
> Each one lays, in his fear and dread.
> Down on the grass his respected head ;
> Each one kicks, as he downward goes,
> Up in the air his respected toes ! "

Then comes the chorus, loud and joyous, from hundreds of voices :

> " So ho ! so ho ! may the courtiers sing,
> Honour and life to Willow the King ! "

Then another fellow in the Eleven gives the next verse, and the captain sings the last, and the chorus again rings through the room, and floats out through the open windows into the warm summer air, startling, perchance, the passing stranger, who wonders what is the cause of the applause that follows the song.

More school songs, more applause, more solos, and then, right heartily given, comes " Auld Lang Syne," sung, with all the time-honoured ceremony, with hands crossed.

Finally comes, from loyal hearts and voices, " God save the Queen ; " and then the fellows pour down the school steps into the yard.

Just by the gates our hero meets Lyon, whom he has not seen till to-day since he left the school. "Hullo, old chap ! how d'ye do ?" he exclaims, grasping his hand ; " what are you about now ? You promised to write often, and you've never given me a line since you left." " Oh, haven't I ? " replied Lyon, carelessly ; "I'm very sorry, but I've been so awfully busy; going in for Sandhurst soon; I've been hard at work ever since I left. But tell us something about yourself, old fellow; you're leaving this term, aren't you?" "Yes, I'm sorry to say I am," answered Russell, taking Lyon's arm, and walking him off towards the house; "I don't half like it now the time is come. However, it can't be helped.——Why, here is 'Jimmy' Belfield, with a lot of old fellows!" Let us leave them in the midst of their handshaking, and pass over twenty-four hours or so.

Russell was walking along the street, arm in arm with Lyon, who had stayed over Sunday; evening Chapel was just over,—the strains of the old familiar hymn, which is always sung at the end of service on the last Sunday of term, were still ringing in their ears, and Russell thought, as he had never thought before, of the beautiful words of the last verse. "All who here shall meet no more." The words seemed to haunt him. True, he would probably often revisit the old place, and see some of the old faces; but it was not like coming back as a schoolboy. After a few years, his name would sound strange in the ears of a younger school-generation, and if he came down to see the familiar places, unknown faces would stare, and wonder who he was; he would hail with pleasure the recognition of an old servant or tradesman, whom he barely knew by sight when he was at school.

Something of this, but not all, he said to Lyon, who attempted, and, in the end, successfully, to brighten our hero's dismal picture of the future. "Oh, nonsense; you'll meet no end of old fellows up at Oxford, and you'll often be down here for

cricket and football; and as to you're not being
known in a year or two, it's all bosh ; and even if it
weren't, you wouldn't mind it *then*.   There's no good
looking so glum about it.   You know, if you stayed
on here much longer, all your friends would leave,
and you wouldn't care much for the new set that
sprang up; I shouldn't bother my head about it, if
I were you."

With such arguments, Lyon enticed Russell from
his gloomy frame of mind; and, soon after, falling
in with several other fellows, the subject dropped,
and was forgotten.

All next day Russell was packing up and running hither and thither.   He had got two "copies,"
and was up at Crossley and Clarke's selecting them,
when he remembered that it was time to go up and
be called over.   Then he went down to see the
swimming competition at "Ducker," and then up
the hill again, to settle bills and pack up books, and
a thousand other small nuisances.   So that when
the evening came he was rather tired.   In
"Speecher" he got two prizes, one a "leaving"
book.   The Head Master made a complimentary
little speech, in wishing him well, and the applause
that followed showed unmistakeably our hero's un-
diminished popularity.   Then came some of the
first *partings*, viz., those with the Scotch and Irish
fellows, who were off that evening, and left before
Chapel.

After "lock-up" there was the usual big supper
in hall.   When the viands had been done justice to,
toasts were proposed.   That of "one of those who
are leaving, our most popular Cricket Captain, and
a member of both School Elevens," was soon given

by Mr. Kingsford,—and Russell's response was awaited amid thunders of applause. Though perhaps neither original nor fluent, it was a fair sample of schoolboy oratory, and ran somewhat as follows:—

" Ladies and gentlemen (laughter)—I mean gentlemen (continued applause),—I am—(applause)—I am very much obliged to you (thunders of applause) for the very kind way in which you have drunk my health. (Hear, hear!) I am very sorry I'm leaving, but I hope that—(hear, hear) that I (applause, and sound of breaking wine-glasses, during which the speaker made a fresh start). I want to express my thanks to Mr. and Mrs. Kingsford for their kindness while I've been here (great applause). I hope the House Cricket Eleven will keep up its name next year, and that we shall be cock-house again. I am sure that the gentleman on my right (great applause) will prove a better captain than I have been (no, no, and applause; more broken glass). There are times, gentlemen, when,—(hear, hear, and laughter) when a fellow doesn't know what to say (laughter and cheers), so I'd better sit down, and give the toast of the future Captain of the Cricket Eleven, Mr. Parry (loud applause, and more glass broken), coupled with success (hear, hear) to the House Cricket." (Loud and continued applause.) Here Russell sat down, overcome by the efforts of his oration, but was soon laughing and applauding the speech of "Mr." Parry, who seemed at a loss what to say, and upset his glass of wine in his nervous efforts to make *some* sound—good, bad, or indifferent.

The speeches, it must be confessed, rather deteriorated as the evening wore on, for all that could be said had been said by former speakers; and at length one gentleman whose health had been drunk, had to confess openly that he had nothing to say except the inevitable " thanks—kind manner in which—drunk my health," a sentiment which was getting a trifle hackneyed. So he " called expressive silence to his aid," and everybody, finding that no more fun was to be got out of his neighbours, spontaneously and simultaneously wished the proceedings at an end ; and, after a somewhat awkward pause, Mr. Kingsford rose, and the hall was soon empty.

Russell went to the drawing-room to pay his adieux to Mrs. Kingsford, after which he repaired to his room, and was before long asleep after the fatigues of the day.

There remains but little more to be told. Next morning, as the coach laden with the Harrow Eleven is lost to sight in a cloud of dust, on their way to finish up their season with a pleasant day's cricket at Moor Park, let us leave our hero, still a member of the School Eleven, but actually and indisputably an old Harrovian.

In laying aside his pen, the Author cannot but feel the feeble character of all he has written. But he will be amply repaid if some memory of old days, some half-forgotten custom, some well-known spot, has been, by these humble pages, brought to the minds of any of that numerous and distinguished body,

THE OLD HARROVIANS

in whose hands he would leave this little work.

" What though, in unceasing flow,
  Generations come and go
      O'er Harrow's hill ?
New trees may bloom, old trees grow sere,
Old buildings moulder, new appear,
Yet Harrow, as year rolls on year,
      Is Harrow still."

From " The Tyro."

GLOSSARY

OF SOME OF THE PRINCIPAL WORDS AND USES OF
WORDS PECULIAR TO HARROW.

N.B.—Orthography not guaranteed.

ALLOWS—Weekly pocket-money.

BILL—The calling over the whole school, about every
two hours on holidays and half-holidays.

BILL-BOOK—A list of the school according to forms,
published every term.

BLUE-BOOK—An alphabetical list of the school, published every term.

BOY—A fag. The word used in "calling" (*vide*
Chap. xvii.).

CALL—A roaring or shouting of the word "boy."
Verb. To call "boy."

CAP—*Phrase* "To get one's cap" = "To get into
one's House Cricket Eleven."

COMPUL—Compulsory Football. (This takes place
twice a week on half-holidays in winter term.
The games are now arranged according to the
merits of the players, irrespective of school order
or houses.)

COCK-HOUSE—Champion-house (either at Cricket, Football, Rackets, Gymnasium, *etc.*).

CON—*Noun Substantive.* A construing lesson.
Verb. To construe.
Phrase. "To give a con" = To construe a passage for the benefit of one or more fellows, less wise or less diligent than the construer.

CONTIO—A Latin Oration read by the Head of the school annually before the Governors, and containing allusions to school events during the past year.

COPY—A book, awarded as a sort of minor prize, several of which entitle the holder to a prize proper.

COVERED—*Noun Substantive.* The covered racket-court.

CRICKET-FAGGING—Fielding out for any members of the Eleven or "Sixth-form Game" who are practising. All the lower school are in turn "put on."

DIV—A division. *e.g.,* "French Div.," "German Div."

DUCKER—(Abbreviation of Duck Puddle.) The school bathing-place.

EX or EXEAT—Leave granted once a term from Friday evening to Monday morning.

EX-LETTER—A letter from home or friends to show where the recipient is to spend his "exeat."

EX-PAPER—A paper signed by all the masters with whom a boy has to do. Without this he cannot go for his "exeat."

EXTRA—Extra school, to which fellows are sent as a punishment. The masters in turn preside over it. The time is occupied in copying out Greek or Latin Grammar.

FEZ—(1) The taselled cap of a member of a House Football Eleven.

(2) A member of a House Football Eleven.

FIND—A company of two or more who take breakfast and tea together.

Verb.   To mess together.

FLANNELS—*Phrase* " To get one's flannels " = " To get into the School Football or, (more usually) Cricket Eleven."

FOOTER—Football.

FOURTH-FORM } —Morning prayers at 7. 30 in the
PRAYERS   }   old Fourth-form Room, attended by certain Forms only, owing to want of space.

FROUST—Extra time in bed in the morning on Sundays, Saints-days, and whole holidays.

FROUSTER—An arm chair.

GYM—Gymnasium.

HOT MEAT—The addition to breakfast and tea purchased at a confectioner's.   (In ordering hot meat, several colloquialisms are used—

e.g., " *Six of sausages with* " = 6d. of sausages with potatoes.

" *Two bob of cutlets without* " = 2s. of cutlets without potatoes.)

HOUSE CAP   } —The cap and shirt of the house
HOUSE SHIRT }   colours which any member of the house can and must wear at football, unless he is a "fez," when the " house cap " is discarded in favour of the more honourable "fez."

HOUSE SINGING—The meeting once a week, of one or more houses, for singing school songs, *etc.*

JAMBICS—Iambics.

LINES—A certain number of lines from a Latin or Greek author, to write out as a punishment.

LOCK-UP—The closing of the doors of all the houses in the evening, the time varying according to the season.

NOGGS—The school factotum.

NOTER—A note-book.

PAVVY—Pavilion.

PHILATHLET—(1) The Philathletic Club.
(2) The Philathletic Field.

PHUG—A heated state of the atmosphere.

PHUGGY—Stuffy, close.

PUN—A punishment, usually consisting in writing "lines," but sometimes the translation of a lesson.

PUN-PAPER—Ruled paper, every fifth line being red, used for writing punishments.

PUPE—Pupil Room (*vide* "Tutor").

REMOVE—(1) Certain Forms below the Fifth Form.
(2) Promotion into a higher form.

REP—A portion of an author to be learnt as a repetition.

SANNY—Sanatorium.

SCHOOL—*Phrases* (1) "A School" = a lesson, usually of one hour's duration.
(2) A master is said to "give his form a school," when he excuses them all a certain lesson, and does not require them to come up to school.

SCUM—Much the same as "smug."

SEND UP—A master sometimes sends a boy to the Head Master, usually for punishment, but sometimes "for good."

SICKER—Sick-room, to which fellows are sent when not ill enough to go to the "Sanny."

10

SIGNATURE—A master's signature, excusing a boy work, bill, *etc.*

SKEW—*Noun substantive.* A dunce.

Verb. To fail in a lesson.

SKY—*Verb.* To overthrow at football.

SLAVE-DRIVER—A boy whose duty is to see that the cricket fags go down when their turn comes.

SMUG—An appellation the reverse of complimentary, usually applied to an unpleasant or unpopular fellow.

SPEECHER—(1) The Speech-room.

(2) The assembly of the whole school in Speech-room.

(3) The day on which the annual School Recitations and Festivities take place. This is in Summer term, and must not be confused with Founders' day, later in the year.

SQUASH—(1) Rackets played with a soft india-rubber ball.

(2) A "scrimmage" at football.

STINKS—Under this euphonious term are included Chemistry, Natural Philosophy, Experimental Science, *etc.*

STRAW—A straw hat. These, made very shallow, are the week-day head-gear of the fellows at Harrow, in winter and summer alike.

SUPER—*Verb.* To superannuate.

SWOT—*Noun substantive.* One who devotes all his time to work.

Verb. To employ oneself with school work.

TAILS—The swallow-tail coat worn by the senior fellows in the school.

Teek—Arithmetic.

Tolly—A candle.

Tolly-up—*Verb.* To keep a candle alight at night, after lawful hours, usually to do work by.

Torpids—House matches at football, in which only those play who have not yet completed two years in the school.

Tosh—A footbath.

Trials—Terminal examinations.

Tutor—(This system is said to be borrowed from Eton.) Except in certain cases the house-master is tutor to all in his house. But if he is not a classical master, the fellows in his house attend the " pupil rooms " of the junior masters.

Twig—*Verb.* To detect. *Past participle,* Twug, detected.

Up—*Phrase* " To be up "=" To be in school."

(The) Vaughan—The school library, built to commemorate Dean Vaughan's head mastership.

PRINTED FOR PROVOST AND CO., TAVISTOCK STREET, LONDON, W.C.